Sir William Martin Conway

The Artistic Development of Reynolds and Gainsborough

Two essays

Sir William Martin Conway

The Artistic Development of Reynolds and Gainsborough
Two essays

ISBN/EAN: 9783337418441

Printed in Europe, USA, Canada, Australia, Japan

Cover: Foto ©Andreas Hilbeck / pixelio.de

More available books at **www.hansebooks.com**

THE ARTISTIC DEVELOPMENT

OF

REYNOLDS & GAINSBOROUGH

TWO ESSAYS

BY

WILLIAM MARTIN CONWAY

*Roscoe Professor of Art, University College,
Liverpool.*

WITH ILLUSTRATIONS

LONDON

SEELEY & CO., 46, 47, & 48 ESSEX STREET, STRAND

1886

THE following Essays are the outcome of such weeks of study as the writer was enabled to consecrate to the magnificent Exhibitions held at the Grosvenor Gallery in the early months of the years 1884 and 1885. The published Catalogues of those Exhibitions cannot fail to maintain a permanent place in the literature of English Art. Frequent references have, therefore, been made to them, and the Catalogue numbers have been employed to identify pictures mentioned. The writer has likewise made free use of the ordinary sources of information about the two great artists. He is, of course, especially indebted to Leslie and Taylor's *Life of Reynolds* and Fulcher's *Life of Gainsborough*.

To my Master

SIDNEY COLVIN

LIST OF ILLUSTRATIONS

REYNOLDS

GAINSBOROUGH

SIR JOSHUA REYNOLDS.

(Born 1723; died 1792.)

I.

IT is, perhaps, no matter for surprise that an artist who painted the portraits of Johnson, Goldsmith, Gibbon, Burke, Sheridan, Garrick, Mrs. Siddons, and the great statesmen and leaders of society of both sexes, in a day when Horace Walpole was immortalising them all with his satirical pen, and Boswell was watching their behaviour and noting down their words—it is small matter for surprise that a painter so circumstanced should be remembered, rather on account of the subjects, than the manner of his work. In a general way, indeed, the public has always liked Sir Joshua's pictures; it has delighted in his *naïve* children, worshipped his courtly ladies, and enjoyed his mellow colouring and the rich bloom of texture which he dusted over all. The public has enjoyed all these things in its own way; but, so far, when it has deputed an author to write about Reynolds, he has been charged to hunt among the letters and memoirs

of the last century for tales and legends about the people
who sat to the great master, for accounts of routs and club-
meetings and dinners at which he was present, for stories of
what he said to Johnson and what Johnson said to him, for
minutiæ of the snuff he took and the ear-trumpet he used,
of the size of his carriage and the colour of its panels and its
lining, for plans of his house and lists of his visitors, and of
his visitors' visitors and their friends. It is well enough,
indeed, that a society should be accurately depicted and
brought down to us ; but that has once for all been done
by Walpole and Boswell, and in these days no *Life of
Reynolds* constructed on the lines of the *Life of Johnson*
can be anything but a weak and blurred reflection of an
incomparable original. By all means let us use Reynolds's
portraits to illustrate the letters and memoirs of his day ;
by all means, too, let us find out what manner of man the
painter himself was, and in what manner of company he
moved, and what they thought of him : but let us bear
in mind that, when we have done all this, we have only
prepared the way for what with the greatest English painter
is the matter of highest importance—the consideration of
him *as an artist.*

Now as an artist Reynolds has never yet been studied ;
no written life of him contains even an attempt to trace the
origin and development of his style. What were his powers
and their limitations ? What is his relative greatness when
measured against the greatness of the greatest ? How
does he stand in the company of the Holbeins and Dürers,

REYNOLDS.

Mrs. Siddons as the Tragic Muse.

Tintorets and Raphaels, of the past? Whence, too, did he
derive his powers? and what of them did he communicate to
his successors? How much of the art of to-day is a direct
outcome of his initiative? how much of the initiative of his
contemporaries? What influence did he have on a Gainsborough, a Romney? What effect did they produce upon
him? To these and a hundred similar questions no answer
has yet been attempted. The 'Tragic Muse' sits majestic
upon her throne, gazing with imperial calm into the murky
air, where Crime and Remorse crouch amid the gloom; and
all that the biographers have to tell us is the gossip of the
studio about the model and her sayings and behaviour. We
want to know that indeed, but we want to know much more.
Whence came that gloomy background and that mysterious
light? Were there not Rembrandts and other great ones
long gone by? and is it not to them that we must look for an
answer? Is the royal Muse Mrs. Siddons only? Could
everybody have beheld Mrs. Siddons so? Or is it not that
she was thus visible alone to eyes long trained to behold in
the men and women of the everyday world the signs of
majesty, power, and tenderness, that we, of the blinder sort,
scarce suspect, any more than we do the brilliant colours of
the stars? Now, however, that public attention has again
been directed to Reynolds, by the noble collection of the
master's pictures recently brought together at the Grosvenor
Gallery, it may not be inopportune to point out certain
general principles and lines of development of Sir Joshua's
art.

II.

HE was a South Devon man, as all the world knows, born
betwixt the moorland and the sea, in the little provincial
borough of Plympton Earl. The picture-books of his childhood, as we shall note, remained all his life long in his
memory, and suggested some even of his later works; but
no such trace is ever found of the granite hills, amongst
which as a lad he must have roamed, or the changeful sea
by whose shore he must so often have played. Nature was
never his book, but the face of man and woman alone. Not
the granite precipice, but the lofty forehead; not the sea-
hollowed cave, but the overhanging brow; not the riven
hillside, but the furrowed cheek; not withered foliage, but
blanched locks of hair; not the wide landscape, in sunshine
and shade, in storm and calm, in summer and winter, but
humanity, joyous or sad, angry or peaceful, in youth or in
age, was the subject of all his study, the goal of his aims,
and itself his 'exceeding great reward.'

It was well for him, then, that he was born at a day
when, in the natural course of things, the individual stood out
so clearly from the surrounding multitude. His life was
passed in a time of war, when generals and admirals were
men versed in battles and famous among their fellows, when
the foundations of an empire were laid by valiant men in one
hemisphere, whilst they were being broken up in another;
when merchants were growing wealthy, and country squires
were not shut out from intelligence and fame; when the

government was in the hands of an oligarchy, the members of which were, at all events, conscious of their own individuality, and proud of their intelligence and knowledge of the world ; and when society, such as we now know it, was being formed, and individuals could shine by social qualities. Everywhere the force of circumstances brought the individual into pro- minence. Men of letters were beginning to take rank as a class, and their faces were familiar to the world. Men of action were needed, and known on all hands. The world of fashion was witty, and prided itself upon its culture and refinement. Whether for good or evil, fame was everywhere ready to carry far the glory of success. In such a day portrait-painting must of necessity flourish ; how, indeed, would it not flourish to-day if photography had not been invented ? Just as in the sixteenth century, when the first great commercial epoch of modern history culminated, and before the wars that succeeded the Reformation had para- lysed industry on every hand, portrait-painting attained its first great measure of success, and called into existence its Holbeins, its Clouets, and its Tintorets, to raise lasting memorials of the men who, in the strife of things, attained pre-eminence among their fellows : so, again, in the time that intervened between the opening of the modern com- mercial epoch and the invention of photography similar causes produced like results. A large number of portrait- painters found employment ; and from amongst them the great ones rose above the level of the men of the same class in years of less active production. Young Joshua having, as

a boy, showed some talent for drawing, his father, the clergy-
man-schoolmaster, readily agreed to his adopting the career
of a painter; knowing that, if only moderately successful, he
would certainly be able thus to earn his daily bread.

The factors that went to form the boy's early style were
few and simple. He was evidently an original child in this
sense, that by inheritance and education he was ever eager to
make trial of new methods, and to strike out new lines. At
school he drew on the back of a Latin exercise not the
commonplace production of youthful genius—a horse, or a
cow, or a schoolfellow—but a perspective diagram, in accord-
ance with rules laid down in a book he had read; so that the
father's criticism on the work was hardly justified, ' This is
drawn by Joshua in school out of pure idleness.' His own
native gift, coupled with his own native industry, led him
forward steadily enough. He copied such prints and
drawings as came in his way—the engravings in Dryden's
edition of *Plutarch's Lives* and the prints in Jacob Cats'
Book of Emblems; and so deeply did some of these subjects
sink into his mind, that when, in his years of greatest maturity, he painted for Boydell the caldron scene in *Macbeth,*
he founded his composition upon that of one of the prints in
the picture-book of his childhood.

At the age of eighteen, then, he had attained a certain
skill of hand; sufficient, at any rate, to warrant his being
bound apprentice to Hudson, who was at that time the recognised leader amongst English portrait-painters. Hudson,
pupil and son-in-law to Richardson, was likewise a Devon-

shire man. His style is thus referred to by Tom Taylor :—
'Every one who is conversant with English country-houses
knows Hudson's style—his inanimate, wooden men, in velvet
and embroidery, and periwig or bob, one hand on the hip, the
other in the waistcoat ; the ladies almost as unvarying, generally half-lengths, in white satin, with coloured bows and
breast-knots, or in flounced brocades, with deep lace ruffles.
Hudson painted solidly and simply, however ; and his men
and women, if tame, are correctly drawn.' He was, in fact,
the best painter of a bad time, his style being much the same
as that of all his contemporaries—a faded remnant of the
style of the Van Dyck imitators, who had flourished in
England since the Restoration.

With this dull but correct man the youthful Joshua was
brought in contact, and soon he learnt from him all he had
to teach. In a few months Reynolds left his master, and
started for himself; his paintings of this period are, it
is plain to see, done under Hudson's influence. The
experimenting tendency of the youth always makes itself
apparent ; but, so far, he does not venture much in new
paths. His works are marked by great taking of pains :
the brush is handled not without a certain hesitation ; the
surface of the picture is wrought very even ; from point to
point the colours are melted together ; there is no attempt
at breadth or boldness of handling. The young artist is,
above all things, eager that whatever he paints shall be right
rather than effective. His pictures are primarily to be true
likenesses. He places his sitter in a perfectly simple posi-

tion, seeking for no charm or strangeness of pose or apparel ;
he then sets to work to draw the features aright, and, above
all things, to catch the character of the face. Down to his
latest days he was a master in the rendering of character ;
and he attained his mastery, not because of any particular
native gift, but by long training of eye, and hand, and
memory. The eye can be trained to see, the memory to
retain, and the hand to trace, whatsoever may be required.
Reynolds from the first laboured after character, looked for
it, fixed it in his memory, and wrought and re-wrought at the
rendering of it, so that he became rewarded by continually
increasing certainty and rapidity of success.

Arrived, then, at this point, he was brought away from
London by his father's death towards the end of the year
1746, he being then twenty-three years of age. He now
settled in a house at Plymouth Dock, where he maintained
himself by his brush, and rapidly began to form relations
with the principal people in the neighbourhood. The importance, however, of his removal to Plymouth lay in the
fact that he was there brought in contact with the paintings
of William Gandy of Exeter. This William Gandy's father
was a pupil and imitator of Van Dyck, but the son did not
adhere to the father's style. His works are forcible, and
often marked by a strong chiaroscuro, and it was by them,
no doubt, that Reynolds was first brought in contact with
the masculine genius of Rembrandt. It is reported that a
great impression was made upon him by Gandy's remark,
that ' a picture ought to have a richness in its texture, as if

the colours had been composed of cream or cheese, and the reverse of a hard and husky or dry manner.' At all events, the study of Gandy's works produced a great effect upon our artist, and may be said to have afforded the impulse which finally decided his line of advance.

The name of Van Dyck must, from his earliest years, have been one of great weight with Reynolds. Unfortunately we do not know what opportunities he had, at the beginning of his career, of seeing the works of that master; upon this point his sketch-books would undoubtedly throw much light, were they only investigated with due care. Throughout the whole of his life he was continually returning to Van Dyck, now and again actually copying his pictures with affectionate care, now and again openly imitating him in arrangement, colouring, or costume. It is clear that this predilection for Van Dyck arose very early in Reynolds; and it was natural that it should, for Van Dyck was the father of modern English portrait-painting. The years that he spent in England (1632–1641) were years of great importance for the history of English art. The works that he then painted formed the canon of later artists, and every English painter for more than a century aimed at imitating them, though with continually decreasing success. It was natural, therefore, that Reynolds, from his boyhood, should have been at all times ready to study the works of this great master; and that he did so is proved not only by his own paintings, but by his direct statements and recommendations to others.

III.

At the beginning of 1749, being then twenty-six years of age, Reynolds started away from England for a journey which lasted over three years, the greater part of the time being spent in Italy. When he started the chief factors of his style, as we have shown, were drawn from the following sources : his own native talent and boyish practice, and the influences of Hudson, Gandy, and Van Dyck, that of the last-mentioned being as yet scarcely traceable. He painted several portraits on his way out, in the ship of his friend Keppel, and at the places in the Mediterranean where he landed ; but we need not now be concerned with these. He then spent two years at Rome, two months at Florence, a fortnight at Bologna, a few days at Parma and other intermediate places, and nearly a month at Venice, whence he returned to London, stopping a month at Paris on the way. Probably most of his Italian sketch-books and note-books remain, and it is in them that the real student of Reynolds will have to search, if he is ever to place before us the true story of the development of the artist. Two of these books are in the British Museum and two in the Soane Museum; Mr. R. Gwatkin also possessed one, and others belonged to Mr. Lenox of New York.

The pictures that he copied and studied were of so many schools and dates (always, however, after the year 1500), that it is impossible to gather from the notes accessible in print what masters *influenced* him above the rest. A comparison of his sketches with his later works will alone bring this to light, and that comparison is one upon which we have not been able to enter. At Venice, however, it is plain that Tintoret and Paul Veronese attracted him most; he admired Titian at all times, but his notes upon that master's pictures are not numerous. He was, it would seem, chiefly interested in observing the methods of distributing light employed by his various fore-runners, and one of his Venetian notes indicates his mode of study. 'The method I took,' he says, 'to avail myself of their principles was this :—When I observed an extraordinary effect of light and shade in any (Venetian) picture, I took a leaf out of my pocket-book and darkened every part of it in the same gradation of light and shade as the picture, leaving the white paper untouched to represent the light, and this without any attention to the subject or to the drawing of the figures. A few trials of this kind will be sufficient to give their conduct in the management of their lights. After a few experiments I found the paper blotted nearly alike. Their general practice appeared to be to allow not above a quarter of the picture for the light, including in this portion both the principal and secondary lights, another quarter to be kept as dark as possible, and the remaining half kept in mezzotint or half shadow. Rubens appears to have admitted rather more light than a quarter, and Rembrandt much less, scarcely an eighth ; but it costs too much, the rest of the picture is sacrificed to this one object.'

An examination of the pictures in the Grosvenor Exhibition seemed to show that, shortly after Reynolds's return from Italy, the influence of Correggio was strongest upon him, but that Tintoret's influence was most permanent. It was likewise easy to find, amongst his earlier post-Italian works, proofs of the attention he continued to pay to the handling of light. The picture painted about 1754 of Lord Cathcart, with the ' Fontenoy scar' (Grosv. No. 137), is a conspicuous instance in point; he is shown standing at a balcony with a background of curtains and Italian architecture, the light striking down behind him through a window on the left. The whole picture is solidified by light, and it is easy to see that the effects are all the result of careful consideration.

Reynolds soon abandoned such attempts, and contented himself instead with plain brown or else open-air landscape backgrounds; but in his sketch-portrait of Lord Bute, of 1763 (Grosv. No. 59), he adopted exactly the same arrangement of curtains, architecture, and light, as in the ' Cathcart' of 1754. Probably, in the first instance, it was the influence of Rembrandt that led Reynolds to undertake this long course of chiaroscuro study; at all events, what may be called his first Rembrandt period was simultaneous with his Italian tour, if the evidence of two pictures can be trusted— the portrait of Wilton, painted at Florence in 1752, and that of Giuseppe Marchi of the following year.* In the picture

* Both of these were exhibited at the Winter Exhibition of Old Masters at the Royal Academy in 1884 (Nos. 51 and 208).

of his servant Marchi. Reynolds directly imitated Rembrandt, not alone in the treatment of the lights, but in the costume—the rich red coat and the glittering turban. The portrait of Wilton is of the same kind. After Reynolds had been a short time in England the Rembrandt influence became less strong, and that of the Italians, and particularly Correggio, took its place.

IV.

WHEN, in 1753, Reynolds settled down to spend the rest of his life in London, he had certainly carried out his father's sound advice, 'never to be in too great a hurry to show yourself to the world, but lay in first of all as strong a foundation of learning and knowledge as possible.' He was now ready to take rank as the leading portrait-painter in England, and the work that proclaimed him such to the world, at the age of thirty, was his full-length portrait of the friend in whose ship he had started on his tour, Commodore Keppel (Grosv. No. 181). The Commodore is depicted walking forward along the rock-bound shore of a stormy sea. His right hand is extended, and his face, brightly expressive, is turned in the same direction. His hair and coat are blown about by the wind. The light strikes downwards upon the figure from the right in rather a mysterious manner, somewhat as Tintoret might have made it. The picture has darkened much with age, but must always have been one in which light took the lead

of colour. There is little colour in it, indeed, only certain
warm flesh-tints and the blue of the sleeve; the rest is in
grey monochrome. Here, however, Reynolds shows his
mastery in catching not the expression of the face only,
but that of the figure too. The effect of walking forwards
is excellently rendered, and, moreover, the man is walking
forward in his own peculiar fashion. There is character
in the tread of the foot, in the pose of the body, in the
gestures of the hands, and the holding of the head. The
man, from head to foot, is all there. If we ask what
influences of other masters can be traced in the work,
we shall find it difficult to render a satisfactory answer.
Reynolds returned from Italy, even as Dürer, still himself.
He had studied much ; he had assimilated much ; but his
studies had not been bounded by any particular limits. He
had assimilated whatever he found in any quarter that was
worthy of assimilation. Traces of Rembrandt, of Tintoret,
of Correggio, perhaps of Van Dyck also, and many more,
might be discovered in this portrait ; but as a work of
art it belongs to no particular school, and could have
emanated from none except that which Reynolds himself
was founding.

When we spoke of the years 1749–1753 as comprising
his first Rembrandt period, we did not mean to imply that
during that time our artist was working exclusively under
Rembrandt's influence. Reynolds never, after he arrived
at maturity, adopted one style exclusively. Gainsborough's
forcible rather than elegant remark, ' D —— him ! how

various he is !' has probably been re-echoed by more than one puzzled student of the master's works. For it often happens that two pictures painted by him simultaneously, are as different in every respect—in style of colouring, in texture, in the treatment of light, and in conception (that is to say, in the manner the artist looked at his subject)—as if they had been the work of different men widely separated both by distance and time. Thus side by side with his Rembrandtesque pictures, he produced others of an altogether different character, experimenting now in one direction and now in another, elaborating various styles which he adopted for awhile, then abandoned, and then, perhaps after many years, suddenly returned to again. Of this changefulness it is impossible to give examples now, for it is only with the pictures before us that we could hope to make ourselves understood. It must, however, be manifest to everyone, that the chronological arrangement of the master's pictures, few of which are either signed or dated, is thus rendered a matter of considerable difficulty, where the note-books and account-books do not help us.

The portrait of Keppel, as has been remarked, made Reynolds's fame, and he was soon fully employed by men of every rank and station capable of commanding his services. He did not spare himself, but worked with extraordinary vigour, as is sufficiently shown by the fact that in the year 1755 alone one hundred and twenty persons sat to him for their portraits. Manifestly all these pictures could not have been done wholly by his own hand. He always had one or more journeymen in his employ, and his practice seems to have been to begin by himself painting the face, and sketching in the background and drapery, then to hand the canvas over to a journeyman, who carried out his instructions as to these accessories; finally he went over the work himself, glazing in the finishing touches, and thus bringing the whole into harmony. It is marvellous, notwithstanding this mode of proceeding, which was customary at the day, how completely Reynolds impressed his own individuality on to, apparently, every inch of the paintings that left his studio.

V.

THUS far our work has been comparatively simple, for the line of the artist's development has been single and not hard to follow. From this point, however, various lines have to be traced simultaneously, and they cross and recross one another in the most confusing fashion. We may divide Reynolds's pictures into the following classes : groups, whole-length figures of men, whole-length figures of women, three-quarter-length men, three-quarter-length women, half-length men, half-length women, heads, pictures of children, pictures of a mother and her child, and ideal pictures. This classification is more scientific than would seem probable to a mere reader. A brief inspection of the pictures themselves is enough to show that for every form of picture Reynolds

REYNOLDS.

Lady Cockburn and her Children.

developed a separate style.   It is fairly obvious, for example,
that all his half-length ladies are painted by one artist; it is
likewise clear that all the ladies' full-lengths come from a
single source; but a spectator might well be forgiven for
imagining that the half-lengths and the full-lengths were
by different men. We cannot, of course, attempt now to
trace the growth and changes of all these different styles,
it shall be sufficient if we take one or two groups of works
as examples of the rest.

   The full-length portraits of ladies form, perhaps, the
most clearly defined class by themselves.   It is probable
that Sir Joshua looked upon these as his greatest works,
at all events in portraiture. They present many points of
peculiarity of treatment, all of which may be summed up in
the statement that they are not pictures of women, but
of nymphs. In Reynolds's fourth Discourse, delivered as
President of the Royal Academy, he makes the following
statement, which is important in the present connexion.
'On the whole,' he says, 'it seems to me that there is but
one presiding principle which regulates and gives stability
to every art. The works, whether of poets, painters,
moralists, or historians, which are built upon general nature,
live for ever; while those which depend for their existence
on particular customs and habits, a partial view of nature,
or the fluctuations of fashion, can only be coeval with that
which first raised them from obscurity.' This statement
contains an element of truth; for it is certain that, when
an artist devotes himself to the representation of humanity,

C

pure and simple, as he beholds it before his eyes, he bases his art upon a foundation which endures for ever and extends to the ends of the earth.

But Sir Joshua did not so understand himself. He thought that when he painted men, women, and children, as they were, in their own clothes of every day, busied about their little every-day affairs, he was painting pictures founded, not upon *general nature*, but on the fluctuations of fashion. He conceived that a portrait of the higher kind should be carried out of the atmosphere of fashion, that the lady should be dressed not in her wonted garments, but in some generalised drapery—'drapery,' as he said, 'and nothing more;' that her occupation should be of a general kind, and not belonging to a particular day; that her character should be the character of the female sex in general, not that proper to a particular person of a particular rank. There was an element of truth in this, and his theory would have been strong for good had it led him to forget everything in the one great fact of humanity, had it led him to look at each woman for the sake of her womanliness and nothing more, to pierce into that, penetrate it to the last secret of character, and set down the tender woman as tender, the true of heart as true, the pure as pure, the wanton as wanton. Sir Joshua did this, indeed, but only when he forgot his theory, and that was seldom in the case of full-length portraits of women.

Take, as example, the picture of Elizabeth Gunning as Duchess of Hamilton. Who knows not the fame of the

Gunnings ? the rage they caused, almost unbelievable in these days; peers and peeresses scrambling on to tables and chairs at Court to get a glimpse of them ? Certainly they must have possessed extraordinary attractions of some kind, over and above a high order of mere beauty. Of all this, however, Sir Joshua gives us no hint in the picture of the year 1758 (Grosv. No. 26). The lady, larger than life, stands in the open air, resting against a sculptured marble pedestal; she is dressed in long, sweeping, clinging drapery, with an ermine cloak fallen from her shoulders. Black hair waves down over one shoulder, and shows up in strong contrast the ivory-textured skin of face and neck. Everywhere there are sweeping outlines, which flow together in long rhythmic curves from head to feet. In the face, however, delicately though the features are delineated, there is no special character, unless, indeed, a general languor about the whole be accepted as such.

It is not, indeed, the picture of a woman. This nymph in her impossible garments, what is she doing out there in the forest, and how did that sculptured marble thing come there ? A glance shows that the whole is an impossibility ; it is not a realised fact, but an illustration to some eighteenth-century Poem or Romance. Its atmosphere is the atmosphere of Rasselas, let us say, but you cannot transport human beings into such a world without completely obliterating their humanity. Sir Joshua would have told you that he was trying to represent the lady not in her own particular surroundings, but removed to a sphere where the particular was merged into the general. As a matter of fact, he was doing what a man must always do if he attempts hypocrisy of that kind ; he was founding his work, not upon nature and fact, but upon the *taste* of a day. He was making of a real woman the kind of nymph that fashion then liked her minstrels to sing about, with such little voices as fashion's minstrels usually possess.

There is no such thing as *general nature.* If you abandon one set of particulars you must adopt another ; and Reynolds made the miserable exchange of an actual world of fact, in which many a noble one still found it possible to act with uprightness and truth, for an impossible world of diseased fancy, existing only for a dilettanti clique in a dilettanti day. It is in this style that the full-length portraits of ladies are painted. Now and again an exceptionally human picture appears, such as that of Lady Glandore, of 1779 (Acad. 1884, No. 148), but these only serve to bring out the peculiarities of the rest by contrast. In the famous 'Mrs. Pelham feeding Chickens,' of 1770 (Grosv. No. 9), the human element likewise predominates, and it is to this fact that the picture owes its popularity. There is nothing general about the chickens, or the farmhouse, or the simple flowered chintz frock ; and if only the lady were more concerned with the fowls and less with the spectator, or rather with her effect upon him, the work would be one of Sir Joshua's best.

It would be easy to say much of the development of this nymph style ; for, like all Sir Joshua's styles, it has its periods

and its stages.. The Duchess of Buccleuch, of 1772 (Grosv.
No. 41), is perhaps one of the least pleasing of all ; for the
proud lady, in her ermine and yellow and white, sitting on a
rustic seat against a tree, in the branches of which hangs a
huge, useless red curtain, is about as unnaturally circumstanced and unhuman as can possibly be. The best of the
set is the picture of Mrs. Thrale and her daughter, of 1781
(Grosv. No. 127), and it is not difficult to see why. Mrs.
Thrale was a woman so completely fashioned according to
the *taste* of her day, that she became little more than the
incarnation of it. She lived, as far as she could, up to the
standard of a nymph. Her ideas, her manners, her mode of
life, were artificial. Thus Reynolds, in painting her and her
daughter in their flowing silk drapery, seated nymph-like in
the woods, painted them in their own characters, or rather in
the characters they were continually striving to assume.

VI.

To this group of full-lengths the half-lengths of ladies form
the strongest possible contrast. For some reason or other,
Sir Joshua never strove, in them, after the same kind of
generalisation. He perhaps looked upon the half-lengths as
works of less importance ; at all events, he was satisfied in
them to take his subject as he found her, and to set her down
so, to the best of his great power. Hence it is these same
half-lengths that form the best class of his works. In them
his rare insight into character, his excellent feeling for femi-

nine grace, his felicity in the attainment of all wealth of colour, brightness of light, warmth of shadow, and richness of texture find unbounded scope. . Moreover, he unconsciously betrays the important fact, that he derived more genuine pleasure from work of this kind, than from the more pompous ideal pictures which the taste of his day forced him to consider greater art. For, from the very first, it is clear that upon these less pretentious paintings he lavished greater and happier pains than upon his large full-lengths ; all of which are much more swiftly painted, and carried to a far less complete point of finish.

One of the earliest of the half-lengths, for instance, is the Mrs. Field, of 1748 (Grosv. No. 195), already referred to. In that the painful care of the young artist is apparent to the most casual spectator. The Lady Caroline Keppel, of 1755 (Grosv. No. 123), shows remarkable progress. She is full-face, leaning forward, and resting on a table with her arms folded. The position, therefore, is one of repose, easily maintained for a long period ; and the artist accordingly set himself to catch the expression of the face to the last point of truth, and he has succeeded in fixing for ever the subdued smile and happy glance of a countenance more than ordinarily amiable. As in all the works of this early period (except the full-lengths), one of the chief characteristics is the care with which the face is modelled. Cheeks and brows are rounded into definite solid form ; and that not by any trick of handling, but by thoughtful labour, every stroke of the brush being laid with fixed intention and producing a corresponding

REYNOLDS.

Pickaback.   Mrs. Payne Gallwey.

effect. Moreover, the traces of the brush are not individually discoverable, but are carefully wrought one into
another, the whole surface being rendered smooth as enamel.
Such is, again, the case with the three-quarter length Lady
Holland, of 1758 (Grosv. No. 74), a picture which belongs
inseparably to this group.   She is seated full-face, working at
a piece of embroidery ; and the picture is specially remarkable because it shows once again the great line of Reynolds's
advance, namely, his steadily increasing power in repre-
senting people as alive.   Here the lady is full of animation
in the truest sense ; she has dropped her hands and work
into her lap, whilst she looks brightly forward at the spectator, and in a moment her lips will open with words of
kindly greeting.   Her quick intelligence and capacious sympathies are clearly visible, and yet there is nothing forced
into prominence ; the work is so good because it is so modest
and unpretending.   The artist wins his greatest praise when
he forgets himself and his theories, and lets his subject live
in his stead ; for in painting, as in everything else, ' he that
loseth his life shall find it.'

Thus far Reynolds had found his powers fully occupied
by the attempt to render truly the best expression and most
characteristic posture in rest of the person before him ; but
after the year 1760, we cannot fail to observe that his loyal
veracity begins to earn an increasing reward.   With every
year, as it passes, he may be seen seizing with more certainty
and ease those qualities which before had only been won
by dint of painful toil.   His mind was, therefore, set at

liberty, as it were, to play around his subject. Henceforward, he not only renders the likeness with increasing truth,
but he is for ever adding new charms of light and colour
and texture and tasteful, costume, to the foundation charm
of life. The 'Blue Lady,' of 1761 (Grosv. No. 79), is an
early instance of this new departure. The face is still painted
delicately and modelled with care, but there is a novel boldness in the treatment of the bright blue dress, done probably
enough in rivalry with Gainsborough ; and not only so, but
what is more important, all the colours of the picture are
related harmoniously together—are mutually dependent, like
the notes in a musical chord : and, moreover, that harmony
is the one best fitted to be a setting for the melody upon
which the whole depends—the character, namely, of the
lady herself. From this time forward Sir Joshua advances
unhesitatingly along the lines he had thus laid down. The
charms of the charming Mrs. Abingdon as 'Miss Prue,' of
1764 (Grosv. No. 7), are the same carried to a further stage
of development ; the artfully artless maid is to be read in
every line of the face, and every gesture of shoulder, arm,
and hand. Costume, pose, and all else, are in keeping ; and
the whole is likewise bright and pleasant to the eye in play
of light and chequerwork of colour, from whatever distance
it may be seen.

Passing over another decade, we come to the Mrs. Morris,
of 1775 (Grosv. No. 89), a picture which possesses all the
charms that the heart can desire. Mystery of light and
joy of subdued but harmonious colouring, richness of texture,

rhythm of line, and balance of mass—everything, in fact, that art can accomplish in this kind is there. The work is honest, the finish excellent, the painting of the drapery and that of the skin each equally good in its own way. And over and above all, and without which all else would be nothing worth, the woman is there in the fulness of her humanity, seen into by an eye trained to look, and set down so for ever by a hand trained to describe. With the picture itself before us, it would be interesting to trace out in detail the very subtle manner in which the harmony of tint is attained, the main masses of colour in one part being echoed elsewhere in fainter tones. From this time forward it is hardly possible to speak of Sir Joshua as having progressed. He enlarged the area covered by his styles, he painted works of one kind and another of equally high merit ; but he never surpassed, or could surpass, this perfect work.

The pictures made between 1780 and 1789, in which year he began to lose his eyesight, fall into a class by themselves. None of them are finished with the same care as the Mrs. Morris ; and, if they show progress, it is not in execution, but in insight into character. Progress of that kind Reynolds maintained till the last day he handled a brush. The portraits of the Countess Spencer with a large hat, of 1782 (Grosv. No. 124) ; Miss Fanny Kemble, of 1783 (Grosv. No. 142) ; the Marchioness of Thomond, of 1784 (Grosv. No. 177) ; Lady de Clifford, of 1786 (Grosv. No. 117) ; and, above all, Lady Elizabeth Foster, of 1787 (Grosv. No. 150), are, in every case, superb. In most of them the ladies wear

that widely-frizzed and powdered hair, which no one except a
skilled artist could satisfactorily treat; but this and all other
minor difficulties Sir Joshua overcame without appearing to
feel them. The Lady E. Foster is before a mottled blue
sky, treated (not for the love of it, as sky, but only for the
love of her) as a pleasant and harmonious background to her
charming face, gentle and rather coy, as it is, with its sweet
smile, half grave, half gay, and the eyes so large and dark,
sunk in the liquid shadows that lurk beneath arched and
gracious brows. It is a most beautiful picture, and yet the
lady is not herself very beautiful; there are many faults of
form about the mouth and elsewhere. Reynolds, however,
has seen further than the mere forms of the face at rest.
He has animated it with the fair expression of a beautiful
mind; he has set it amidst such surroundings of colour
and costume as were best and most expressive; and by so
doing, he has shed over it a larger and nobler beauty than
any chill accuracy of sculpturesque forms could have possessed; he has demanded of the admiring spectator the
exercise of higher qualities of admiration than those which
arise from the sight of merely animal beauty.

VII.

WE can only treat now of one more type of Sir Joshua
Reynolds's works, and that being so, we will confine our
attention to his portraits and pictures of Children. It was
but natural that, immediately after his return from Italy,

REYNOLDS.

Lavinia Bingham, afterwards the Countess Spencer

he should be haunted with the memory of a multitude of
pictures of the Virgin and Child, which had formed a main
part of the subjects of his study for so long. The pictures
of a mother and her babe, so many of which he afterwards
painted, are all more or less impregnated with the old
religious spirit, thus unconsciously revived. One of the
first of the kind is the portrait of Lady Cathcart and her
child, of 1755 (Grosv. No. 71), and in this Italian influence
is most unmistakable. The mother sits uprightly, with a
kindly glance from her eyes, indeed, but still with much of
the dignity of a Madonna. The child is rather an echo
from a picture than a study from the life. It is a little
shrinking thing, neither beautiful nor fascinating, scantily
clothed in a manner more suited for Italian sunshine than
English damps. Were it to raise its hand with the gesture
of benediction, the group would be turned at once into a
Virgin and Child of orthodox type. The full-length of
Lady Pollington and her little boy, painted in 1762 (Grosv.
No. 113), is of course a work of totally different kind.
The picture does not belong to the class of nymphs, but
to one we have not yet alluded to, that of people portrayed
for the sake of their robes. Sir Joshua painted a good many
peers and peeresses in this way—two pompous portraits of
the Duke of Cumberland, for instance, and a full-length of
Lady Waldegrave, of 1759 (Grosv. No. 152)—and in
almost every case it is evident that the garments are the
real subject of the picture, whilst the human being beneath
them shrinks into a mere lay figure. An exception to this

apparently almost invariable rule is the three-quarter length portrait of the Marquis of Rockingham in the robes of the Garter, of 1774 (Grosv. No. 162). He alone rises superior to his raiment, and by his brightly intelligent face, full of other thoughts than those of his own appearance, attracts the attention of the spectator away from the fluttering glories of his attire. Lady Pollington, however, is swallowed up in her robes and her coronet, and has no sympathies to spare, if any could possibly be forthcoming, for the little dressed-up doll of a boy who runs along at her feet. The whole picture is one of costume and ceremony, and possesses no human interest whatsoever.

Seven years later, however, we already find the master risen to higher things. In 1769 he painted the charming picture of the Countess Spencer, with her arms round the waist of her child, who stands on a table by her side,* and the still more charming fancy-piece called 'Hope nursing Love' (Acad. 1884, No. 18). Both of these pictures are characterised by that closeness of connexion between the parent and the child, which Reynolds at last succeeded in attaining to so remarkable a degree. It is no longer an upright woman with anybody's child seated upright on her lap; but in these, and in all the later pictures of this type,

---

* Grosv. No. 157. This picture (a three-quarter length) is of special interest because there exists another canvas (Grosv. No. 199), upon which Reynolds had begun to paint the same subject as a half-length, the only difference being that the child is on the other side of her mother. We are thus enabled to watch the commencement and the completion of the work.

REYNOLDS.

Miss Bowles.

mother and child form parts, as it were, of one organism,
smile together with the same thrill of joy, move together
with the same motion, and are wholly and visibly one in
happy life. Of course the most perfect work of the kind
is the famous Duchess of Devonshire and her child, of 1786
(Grosv. No. 81). There, the mother swinging her laughing
babe on her arm, while it tosses up its little hands and kicks
out its little feet in delight, is the incarnation of 'all that
ever was joyous and clear and fresh' upon this earth of
ours. But such a work could not be produced by a young
artist, and was only possible to Reynolds late in life. The
perfect unity which locks together all the little gestures
and expressions of the two, just caught in the midst of
movement and laughter, could only be attained by a man
whose memory was stored with the results of long and
loving study of many such happy incidents in happy family
life.

Of course Sir Joshua's progress in power of painting
Mother and Child depended in great measure, though not
entirely, upon his progress in the painting of Children. It
is perhaps scarcely surprising, but it must not be forgotten,
that this power was one of the latest which Reynolds
acquired. In his early portraits of children he almost
always worked strongly under the influence of other artists,
especially of Van Dyck. It was long before he felt himself
able to stand alone on this most difficult ground. His first
really independent picture of a child was not painted till
1767. It is the picture of Miss Cholmondeley 'crossing the

brook' (Grosv. No. 57). She has tucked up her little petticoats, taken off her little shoes, and picked up her fluffy dog, which she holds stoutly with both arms, almost squeezing the life out of the dismayed beast. This picture is not in the manner of Van Dyck, or any one else, but is pure open-air English, full of the spirit of country life and free, joyous childhood; and the moment Reynolds had caught that spirit he never lost it again. Sometimes, indeed, he goes back to Van Dyck for his costumes and one thing and another—and why should he not?—but the gladness of childhood is the main subject of his picture, and all the rest is visibly a mere tasteful addition.

It would seem that about 1773 he discovered that his power in this line was ripe; at any rate, in that year he painted a great many children with obvious delight—Emilia Vansittart (Grosv. No. 25), for instance, and the 'Strawberry Girl' (Grosv. No. 86), and 'Mrs. Hartley romping with her Child' (Grosv. No. 139). In all of these pictures the foundation of his success is the same; it is the fact that he seeks in each child for the evidences of its character as a child. He shows himself an observer of childish ways; he notes all their little shynesses and coynesses, never trying to draw them out of themselves, or making them behave otherwise than naturally, but catching them in those moments when, of all others, they were most true to themselves. Now and again he forgets that this is the foundation of his strength, and whenever he does so he fails lamentably. The picture of Master Wynn as the Infant St. John (Grosv. No. 18),

REYNOLDS.

Georgiana, Duchess of Devonshire, and her Daughter.

painted in 1776, is a complete failure, and so is the Lord Porchester as Infant Bacchus, among a number of badly stuffed lions, done in the same year (Grosv. No. 76). Whenever, too, he tries his hand at painting a Baby Moses, or a ' Babe with Angels,' or anything of that kind, he attains a less measure of success than in his frankly natural things ; and the same is the case with such pictures as the ' Felina,' the ' Robinetta,' and the ' Muscipula,' in which he tried to infuse into the face of the child something of the character of a bird or a cat. The Infant Hercules, too, strangling serpents in his cradle, failed for a similar reason, and the only exception to this rule (and that is but an apparent exception) is the picture of the Cherubs' Heads in the National Gallery, of 1786. Had Reynolds never been in Italy, and never heard talk, and talked himself about the 'grand style' in painting, he would not have thought of wandering thus off the track that his own delight and his own skill marked clearly out for him. Truth to say, he wandered off it but seldom, and (excepting the Hercules) all the pictures that he painted of ideal children are quickly done and lightly finished, so that he wasted little time over them.

About 1777 he attained maturity as painter of children, and that maturity is marked by the fact that, henceforth his attention is not so much occupied with the difficulties of his ' task, but that he has some to spare for the frolics of his subject. He often paints the little children now as naïvely acting little parts, dressed as grown-up people perhaps, but

always maintaining their childishness supreme. Such a
picture is the inimitable ' Fortune-tellers ' (Grosv. No. 146);
and such, again, is the charming group of the Parker children
(Grosv. No. 145) as a pair of lovers, the little girl sitting
so coyly there while the boy lets his arm creep timidly round
her waist. Another picture, which partakes of somewhat
the same character, is the portrait of the young Duke of
Gloucester, of 1780 (Grosv. No. 53, belonging to Trin.
Coll. Cambridge), standing pompously on the top of a hill
against the blue sky, with his large feathered hat in the
hand that rests on his walking-stick, his fine cloak worn
with such an air, and over it all his little face looking
childishly conscious of the dignity he has already learned
to put on.

At once a companion and a contrast to this is the
maiden known as ' Collina,' painted in the preceding year
(Grosv. No. 153). She stands, in perfect sweetness and
simplicity, on the top of a hillock, with her beautifully
rounded face under a wealth of dark curling hair ; her dress
is tucked up all about her waist, and shows the most dapper
and coy little feet you can possibly imagine. All this, however, will be within the memory of the reader ; it is likewise
only necessary to mention the names of the ' Simplicity ' and
' Innocence,' painted in the years 1787 and 1788, to remind
him how Reynolds developed his powers of dealing with
children up to the very last.

We have thus briefly reviewed Sir Joshua's development
as a painter of children and young girls, but we have said

REYNOLDS.

Master Crewe, in the Costume of Henry VIII.

nothing of his schoolboys. Even a schoolboy can often depict his kind with tolerable force and accuracy; hence it is not surprising that our artist attained success in this line long before he had learnt to depict babies and little girls. His picture of Lord Warwick as a boy, painted in 1756 (Grosv. No. 201), leaves little to be desired. He is a solemn lad, wanting in every trace of the frolicsome boyishness that we afterwards find; but he is a boy all the same, if rather a stupid one. The first really excellent boy's portrait in the Grosvenor Exhibition was that of the young scholar with a big portfolio under his arm, painted in 1777 (No. 192). Out of those large dark eyes, which look full at you from beneath a shaggy thatching of hair, the whole of boy nature brightly glances. There is in them all the latent potentiality of mischief, laughter, quick intelligence, straightforwardness, and all other qualities which characterise the genus. The same observations hold true of the ' Reading Boy,' of 1784 (Grosv. No. 90); though he is more studiously disposed, there is the same undercurrent of frolic and fun visibly present in him.

Youths on the borders of manhood are treated by Sir Joshua in a style of their own. If full-lengths, they are painted in rich costumes of Van Dyck fashion; and these pictures possess much the same qualities as the group of full-length ladies. The half-lengths are far better, and, indeed, it would be difficult to choose three pictures of any single year superior to the three portraits of young men of 1782—to wit, the Duke of Hamilton, aged sixteen (Grosv.

No. 99); 'Vathek' Beckford, aged twenty-one (Grosv. No. 186) ; and Richard Burke, aged twenty-four, but looking some years less (Grosv. No. 93). These three pictures, not alone in richness of colouring, which is common to them all, but in a certain distinction of appearance, a look of good breeding in its truest sense, as well as in richness of life and youthful vigour, clouded indeed in two cases by an affectation of languor, stand above all others that Sir Joshua painted in this kind. They serve as a further signal of the secret of the master's success, which lay, not in any particularly wide compass of intellectual gifts, though in these he was no-wise deficient, nor in any extraordinary diligence, though in that also he did not fail, but in the fact that he applied his gifts and his labour to the right ends. He attacked each subject with true generalship, and arrayed his forces so as to make them tell to the uttermost. In children he looked for the child, in boys for the evidences of boyishness, in maidens for maidenliness, and in men for manliness and the expression of judgment and will. Other artists may have given a more comprehensive embodiment of the all-round character of their subjects, they may have known how to render a greater complexity of expression, but none has succeeded more admirably in catching the tone of a man at a particular moment, catching him in the midst of an action and setting him down thus, with the fire in his eye and the word on his lips ; and this power, to which Reynolds attained, if not the highest and the rarest of all, is still very high and very rare in the annals of art.

THOMAS GAINSBOROUGH.

(Born 1727; died 1788.)

I.

THE story of an artist's life is the explanation of his works. But that story cannot always be told. Changes of abode, the making of new acquaintances, the opening up new fields of study and interest, occurrences of a seemingly accidental nature—these, and the like events, mark definite stages in the growth of some characters, and enable the student to point with certainty to the leading forces by which a man has been moulded and fashioned into greatness. But the growth of other men, destined to attain equal heights, is as the growth of a tree—silent, continuous, and uneventful. They wax steadily from year to year. They are nourished by whatever surrounds them at the time. They make no sudden starts ahead, neither do they linger in their increase. It is the little occurrences that, from moment to moment, make them what they become. You cannot block out their careers into periods. No bold lines of division sunder them for you into epochs. Only the deeds and productions of such men tell the tale of their days, and you may almost neglect the circumstances and events of their environment.

Such a contrast might be drawn between Beato Angelico and Raphael. It is enough to remember about the
former that as a lad he became a Dominican friar; and
that thenceforward he painted in calm seclusion. His
biographers tell us how he lived in this and the other
town at different periods of his life; but his pictures manifest no corresponding changes of style. Such as the youth
was, such also, only more advanced, was the man. If he
studied the works of other painters, he never suffered their
influence to affect the clear statement of his own ideas.
He progressed evenly and continuously on the lines his
own simple character marked out for him; and when he
had done his work, he passed away quietly as he had
come. With Raphael, on the contrary, it is altogether
different. From childhood to maturity he underwent one
new influence after another, and his pictures manifest each
in turn. Now it is Timoteo Viti that he follows, now
Perugino, Lionardo, Fra Bartolommeo, or Michelangelo.
His movements from place to place brought him in contact
with new personalities; and his art always showed the
effects of the atmosphere that surrounded the artist. The
life of such a man admits of being written—a knowledge
of its main features is essential to a proper understanding
of his works; but the life of a Fra Angelico cannot be
written, for it consisted not in outward changes, but in an
inward growth. His pictures themselves tell all, or almost
all, that a student of them requires to know.

In this respect Gainsborough resembles the Dominican

friar, though in this only. The events of his life were
few, and his art was little affected by them. For clearness'
sake they may be set down at this point. Thomas Gainsborough was born in 1727 at Sudbury in Suffolk. His
father was a crape-maker and a dextrous fencer ; his mother
possessed some skill in painting flowers ; his brothers showed
a good deal of mechanical ingenuity ; and the whole family,
Thomas included, were marked by an attractive, harum-
scarum disposition. As a lad the future artist roamed and
sketched about the country round Sudbury. When fourteen
years old he was sent to learn painting in London ; and
he studied there for three years in the St. Martin's Lane
Academy. After an ineffectual attempt to set up for himself
in the metropolis, he returned to Suffolk, married a lady with
200*l.* a-year, and settled down at Ipswich. He removed to
Bath in 1760, and remained there till 1774 ; when he came
to Schomberg House, Pall Mall, London. In 1780 the
musician Fischer ran away with his daughter Mary. In
1783 he made a tour in the Lake District. In the summer
months, during his residence in London, he had lodgings at
Richmond. Finally, in 1788, he went to see the trial of
Warren Hastings, caught cold there, and, after a few months'
sickness, he died, and was buried at Kew.

The man was thoughtlessly generous, impulsive, capri-
cious, uneven. He was a lively, rattling talker, excellent
at repartee. 'The swallow in her airy course never skimmed
a surface so light as Gainsborough touched all subjects ;
that bird could not fear drowning more than he dreaded

deep disquisitions.' He might have had the society of the learned, he preferred that of the frolicsome. He haunted the green-room, loved actors and musicians, and they loved him. He basked in the sunshine of life, and would soon have perished in the shade. He rejoiced in the jolly creed, 'We are all going to heaven, and Van Dyck is of the company.' The book of Nature—thank the gods!—was library enough for him. A sun-carpeted bank of grass was a volume of natural science worth all the philosophy in the world to his merry mood. Music gladdened him, and the play was pleasant in his eyes; but we never hear of his caring for poetry, except in the form of a jovial song.

His natural bent was evident enough ; and no sturdy mentor presided over his youth, to restrain him from whatever waywardness his fancy might decree. On the contrary, fortune handed him over to Hayman, arch-rake and deeply-versed Bohemian ; and under his guidance, at the early age of fifteen, he made acquaintance with the ins and outs of London. From childhood his eye had been open to all fair sights. 'There was not,' as he himself declared, 'a picturesque clump of trees, nor even a single tree of any beauty—no! nor hedgerow, stem, or post,' in or around his native place, which was not fixed in his memory from his very earliest years. The delight of the eye in the fair sights of nature was an inborn passion with him. He did not care to investigate or understand, he loved to gaze. His study of the book of Nature was confined to turning over the pages and looking at the pictures. He rejoiced in the outsides of things if they were prettily formed, prettily coloured, prettily lit, prettily combined. He did not care about meanings or intentions, and neither looked for them in nature nor made them the basis of his art.

The external was his field of labour and delight—the look of nature and the look of man. He did not trouble himself about manifesting one's character in his portrait; he wanted to produce a likeness, and at the same time to paint as pretty a picture as he could. His whole life long he went on endeavouring to make his pictures prettier and prettier. This was his single, all-sufficient aim. He was not the kind of man to try all manner of styles and experiments, as Reynolds did. He was the opposite of Reynolds in almost every respect, except that the two were contemporaneous, and so subject to the governance of the same social and economical forces. Reynolds walked by faith, Gainsborough by sight. Reynolds was under the influence of theory, and was both hindered and helped by tradition and the belief in the 'Grand Style.' Gainsborough was free from every kind of pedantry, good, bad, and indifferent. Reynolds listened to the counsels of poets, historians, men of letters. Gainsborough troubled his head about nothing of the kind. He was a free child of Nature, endowed by birthright with the purest artistic spirit. His great virtue was that he gave that spirit free play, and followed whithersoever its whims and pranks led him. But a truce to generalities! let us look at the works of the youth and the man!

II.

HERE, then, is 'Tom Peartree's Portrait' (Grosv. No. 395) to begin with—a bust of a man leaning his face on his arms, as though looking over a wall; the whole painted on a board, which has been cut away to the outline of the figure. The thing was painted about the time of Gainsborough's pupilage in London, from a sketch made in his boyhood on a well-known occasion. The lad was one day sketching at home in a summer-house, overlooking an orchard, when his eye rested on a man gazing long and intently at the fruit over the orchard wall. Presently he was observed to scale it with thievish intent, but not before the young artist had fixed his lineaments upon one of the pages of his sketch-book. This is the earliest recorded instance of Gainsborough's habit of seizing the subjects chance threw in his way.

A sketch of a boy's head (Grosv. No. 41), painted years afterwards, when Gainsborough was visiting at Burton Grange, near Taunton, is another example of a similar impromptu. Gainsborough had employed a village boy to grind colours for him. 'Returning suddenly to the room, he found the boy assiduously trying to copy something on a piece of board, while looking up intently, as if for artistic inspiration. The artist was so struck by the boy's earnest gaze that, shouting, "Stay as you are!" and catching up a canvas, he immediately dashed off this sketch.'*

* Grosvenor Catalogue, 1885.

Reynolds, in his *Fourteenth Discourse*, from which we shall have to quote more than once, says that Gainsborough 'had a habit of continually remarking to those who happened to be about him whatever peculiarity of countenance, whatever accidental combination of figure, or happy effects of light and shadow, occurred in prospects, in the sky, in walking the streets, or in company. If, in his walks, he found a character that he liked, and whose attendance was to be obtained, he ordered him to his house,' and there painted him from the life. Thus it was that in the last years of his life he picked up Jack Hill among the Richmond woods. The lad proved a bad bargain, but he had a pretty, chubby face, and that was enough for Gainsborough. The impulse of the moment settled every question, and a rosy cheek was irresistible.

He was instinctively rebellious against convention, as all his early sketches show. He took Nature as he found her. When he was a student in London, this unconventionality was by no means in vogue ; whatever teaching Gainsborough received must have been calculated to break down the freedom of his conceptions. Portrait-painting was the only kind of art work much in demand, and for that there were all manner of canons not to be lightly transgressed. The traditions of Kneller were still supreme, and no one had arisen to abolish them. The artificiality of the seventeenth century maintained its hold upon artists till Reynolds and Gainsborough effected a revolution. Both artists in their youth had to submit to those restraints which in after years their strength availed to burst through. The portraits painted by Gainsborough when settled at Ipswich after his return from London, give proof of this. Those of Mr. and Mrs. Hingeston (Grosv. Nos. 94 and 89) may be taken as examples. Both are of the usual type--half-lengths seen within an oval, the face turned in three-quarters to right or left, as the case may be; there is nothing original in pose or the treatment of costume. The work is throughout careful, solid, simple, and unpretentious—full of promise, therefore. Facial expression is happily caught; there is a glance in the eyes, a mobility in the mouth. Yet it is plain to see that Gainsborough did not feel himself free, in these and the like portraits, to do as he liked; he had to adopt the type fixed by custom; his patrons would not yet tolerate any bold innovations. The portrait of his bride (Grosv. No. 108) shows what kind of treatment he would have adopted at this time, if he had had himself only to consult. The picture, though clearly a good likeness, gives no indication of the 'extraordinary beauty' for which Margaret Burr is said to have been famed in the Sudbury district; she looks a plain, bright, chubby, healthy girl, young and jolly, kind-hearted and boisterous, good and capable. Gainsborough could paint her just as he pleased, so he did away with oval frames and plain brown backgrounds, and placed his mistress in the open air. A boldly treated landscape, with a fretwork of large foliage before a sky rich with evening colours, shuts her in behind; tendrils of honeysuckle creep round her arm, as though they would embrace her. Her costume, too, is freely treated ; a white shawl slips from her shoulders, her bosom is partly revealed, her head is bare. Background, textures, garments, expression, all are Gainsborough's own. He has ridden himself of conventionality for the time; he is a free man—he is himself.

An unfinished self-portrait painted about the same date (Grosv. No. 161) would doubtless have shown similar freedom. Only the face is brought to anything like completion, but that is excellent. The young vagabond with his merry glance is visibly before us; he has caught his own expression inimitably. It is a bright, intelligent countenance, not without traces of care, but with a look of potential merriment, before which all gloomy things could not but fade away. About this time he painted two groups of himself and his wife, seated under the open sky. One (Grosv. No. 9*) shows them in some gentleman's park, dressed in their best, in costumes of about the year 1750. The pertness of the little round-faced lady and the jollity of her military-looking husband are unmistakable, but they are both on their good behaviour; the artificial temple in the background throws a shadow of conventionality over them. In the other picture (Grosv. No. 195) they are in the open country, whither they have gone rambling with their child and dog; they have just sat

---

* This picture was described as a portrait of Thomas Sandby in the Grosvenor Catalogue. Mr. Scharf pointed out to me that it was much more probably a portrait of Gainsborough.

down upon the grass by a little pool, and the dog is
drinking at the water. The sky is cloudy (Gainsborough
always painted it so), but what do they care? The wife
is good-tempered as ever, and the husband, wearing the
same three-cornered hat as in his bust portrait mentioned
above, and with his stockings all crooked and his ill-fitting
clothes carried anyhow, looks the very incarnation of easy
going. Fulcher tells a pretty little story about the relations
between the pair. Whenever Gainsborough spoke crossly
to his wife, a remarkably sweet-tempered woman, he would
write a note of repentance, sign it with the name of his
favourite dog 'Fox,' and address it to his Margaret's
pet spaniel 'Tristram.' Fox would take the note in his
mouth, and duly deliver it to Tristram. Margaret would
then answer :—'My own dear Fox, you are always loving
and good, and I am a naughty little female ever to worry
you as I too often do, so we will kiss and say no more
about it. Your own affectionate, TRIS.'

III.

FOR fourteen or fifteen years we must think of Gainsborough as living a happy enough country life, with
Ipswich for centre, and plenty of landscape to sketch and
paint for his artistic, if not his pecuniary advantage. He
surrounded himself with a set of boon companions, and
became known through all the country side as a good
fellow and a good portrait-painter. But he was made for

something more than local fame, and his removal to Bath opened a new and wider sphere for the exercise of his powers.

The change of abode was marked by no change of style ; his development was continuous wherever he was. But he now had a better chance than before, and in the portrait of Earl Nugent (Grosv. No. 204), painted in 1761, he made his first great hit. He showed the stout old gentleman sitting in the corner of a room by the window, content with all the world. The colour harmony of the picture is not by any means perfect. The blues, greens, and reds, are all too shrill ; but the excellent rendering of expression on the round, good-humoured countenance, the way in which the smile is caught in the midst of its growth, the ease, too, of the pose and its obvious naturalness to the sitter—larger virtues like these make amends for much. If we look to find traces of the influence of Van Dyck, the master whose work Gainsborough so highly revered, we shall look in vain. The picture is of pure and simple English type, and resembles a figure taken out of one of those conversation pieces which for the last fifty years had been popular in England. The putting together of the thing, indeed, is not a good example of *style* of any kind. The idea of *style*, of making all the parts of a picture— background, costume, trimmings, accessories of every kind, the pose of the figure, and the general scheme of light and colour—the idea of making all these component parts work together to a single end, had not as yet assumed prominence

in Gainsborough's mind.   At present we find him labouring
away at details, striving to reproduce on his canvas a
suggestion of the thing his eye saw.   It was a problem
sufficiently engrossing.   The first business of a portrait-
painter is to catch the likeness, and likeness-catching, by
all accounts, was Gainsborough's peculiar gift.   We can
well understand that the portrait of Earl Nugent was a
remarkably good and animated reflection of the man himself, and the gay world of Bath were quick to take note
of that fact.   Gainsborough had not yet attained the power
of giving an air of distinction to his sitters ; at present he
contented himself with giving them an air of reality.   He
had not yet begun to flatter, he was struggling after simple
truth.

From this time forward commissions came pouring in in
increasing numbers, and the artist was enabled to raise his
prices to a very respectable level.   He became a well-to-do
man, and could live in the generous, joyous fashion that
suited so well his thoughtless bent.   Idleness and gaiety
may be censurable to some persons, but with Gainsborough
they were virtues, child of nature that he was.   Repression
would have ruined him.   He waxed in stature and power
as an artist, because his nature was not contradicted.   The
law that he was unto himself was a law whose sanctions were
present joy or present grief.   His art was a joyful thing to
him when he followed his own inclinations in it.   Had he
tried to paint as Reynolds did, had he tried to cover the
intellectual ground which Reynolds was always endeavouring

to add to the domain of art, he would have failed, and been unhappy. But he contented himself with the outer — he gave expression to the thing that he saw—and year by year not only did he see more clearly, but the very track of his brush, the technique with which it was handled, became increasingly instinct with expressive power.

A comparison between the full-length portrait of Earl Nugent and that of Mr. Poyntz, painted in the following year, enables us to take a measure of his advance. Conventionality is rapidly giving way. The artist is finding himself self-sufficient. He is occupying with increasing certainty a footing of his own. Mr. Poyntz (Grosv. No. 55) is seen in the open air, leaning against a pollard willow by a stream. His gun is in his hands, and his dog lies panting at his feet. The management of the light, falling in islands upon his face and upon the dog, is a little artificial, but it gives evidence of an advance, and shows that the artist was paying attention to this matter, and in doing so was endeavouring to follow the leading of Van Dyck. The accessories are all painted rapidly and boldly, though with clear reference to nature at every point. Probably Gainsborough took many of them from objects present in his studio.

Reynolds says that Gainsborough was wont to bring from the fields 'into his painting-room stumps of trees, weeds, and animals of various kinds ; and designed them not from memory, but immediately from the objects. He even framed a kind of model of landscapes on his table, composed of broken stones, dried herbs, and pieces ot

looking-glass, which he magnified, and improved into rocks,
trees, and water. . . . It shows the solicitude and extreme
activity which he had about everything that related to his
art; that he wished to have his objects embodied, as it
were, and distinctly before him; that he neglected nothing
which could help his faculties in exercise, and derived hints
from every sort of combination.' 'He made,' says Jackson,
'little laymen for human figures; he modelled his horses
and cows, and knobs of coal sat for rocks; nay, he carried
this so far, that he never chose to paint anything from
invention when he could have the objects themselves. The
limbs of trees which he collected would have made no
inconsiderable wood-rick, and many an ass has been led
into his painting-room.'

To this same period belong five pictures of children,
which, for comparison's sake, shall be grouped all together.
They are 'Johnnie Plumpin' (Grosv. No. 17), 'Edward
Clive' (Grosv. No. 50), 'Susan Gardiner' (Grosv. No. 127),
'Juliet Mott' (Grosv. No. 162), and 'Georgiana Spencer'
(Grosv. No. 184). Johnnie Plumpin's picture looks the
earliest of these. For all I know, it may have been painted
in the Ipswich period. At all events, it is conventional
enough. The boy is hurrying along, in a Van Dyck
costume, carrying books under his arm, on his way to
school. He is looking very bright and enthusiastic about
it all, as a model boy should look, but a real boy certainly
would not.

Edward Clive (then, or afterwards, Earl Powis) is a

GAINSBOROUGH.

Lady Georgiana Spencer, afterwards Duchess of Devonshire,

more human-looking lad. He and his clothes are painted
with an ungrateful set of colours, but made entirely• real
for all that. The posture of the child, curiously enough,
is almost the same as that of the 'Blue Boy.' The bright
expression of his face is quite wonderfully caught. There
is a lurking look of mischief in his eyes, and altogether he
is a thoroughly natural boy, emancipated from every trace
of Knellerism.

Georgiana Spencer, destined to be Duchess of Devonshire, shall be taken as representative of the three little'
girls. Her picture must have been painted about 1763
or 1764. There is nothing original about her pose. She
has been asked to stand still and upright, as a good little
girl should, with her hands crossed on her waist. The
painter has just set her down as she looked, her quaint
little face peering out of a white cap with pink bows.
Such a bright, laughter-loving little face it is, the merriest
of eyes presiding over a button of a turned-up nose.
She is as full of character as can be—the quaintest of
children !

Probably her father's portrait (Grosv. No. 16), a half-
length within a brown oval, was painted about the same
time. Like all Gainsborough's pictures of this period, it is
not attractive at the first glance, but it is as fine a piece
of character-painting as he ever did. Indeed, as he advanced
in power his portraits grew less remarkable in this very
respect. He attained increasing skill in catching expression,
but he ceased to labour after that complete rendering of

E

character which can only be effected by long and close observation, unless the artist possesses a natural insight of a kind that was not consonant with Gainsborough's endowments and disposition. Reynolds advanced from year to year as a painter of character. Gainsborough became more and more a painter of expression. The two things are connected, but they are not the same, and the student of portrait-painting must not fail to make clear in his own mind the distinction between them.

A portrait which thoroughly renders a man's character is a portrait of the monumental kind, allied to sculpture. Expression is undoubtedly the quality which a painter is specially called upon to catch, and in the seizing of it he manifests, in all their freshness, the resources and flexibility of his craft. Though it is not to be supposed that Gainsborough analysed and formulated the question in his own mind, his instinct guided him in the right direction. Pleased, as he by nature was, with the outward glance and momentary aspect of things, with the joyous shimmer of a universe of change, he could not but emphasise in his rendering of a face that very quality which was for him the leading charm and fascination of the visible world—and what did he care for the invisible? It was the clearness and sharpness of Gainsborough's limitations, and the willing obedience with which he conformed to them, that enabled him to be so perfect an artist in his own sphere. But we are now considering the paintings done by him in the struggling period of his life. As yet he is only an artist of promise; it is not

GAINSBOROUGH.

Orpin, Parish Clerk of Bradford, Wilts.

clear what he will become—Time, the revealer, is steadily
working for us.

About this time he painted the life-size family group of
the Dehanys and their child (Grosv. Nos. 176), whilst the
portrait of the Cruttenden girls (Grosv. No. 61) was perhaps
done a little earlier. Both pictures show that the artist had
not yet learnt how to combine figures together. The individuals are only juxtaposed. They are not united. We can
observe in them the reiterated attempt to handle light effec-
tively and make it subservient to the general effect; we can
see traces in them of the painter's struggle with textures,
his endeavour to give glossiness to silk and fluffiness to
trimmings; as yet, however, he attains only partial success.
In one thing he never fails; he makes every face animated
and bright. The spectator cannot doubt but that he is looking
at a good likeness. Now and again, perhaps, the result
seems to have been reached by a lucky chance, but usually
honest hard work was the foundation of success. The half-
length of Mrs. Walker (Grosv. No. 39), for instance, is
almost Holbeinesque in its elaborate modelling and finished
surface. It is a complete and solid piece of work. There
is much variety in the costume (all the parts of which are
well imitated), and the light is so directed that the beholder cannot help looking chiefly at the face, whereunto
all the rest of the picture is, as it should be, confessedly
accessory. But we have lingered too long over this intro-
ductory stage of our inquiry, and now Kilmorey's erect and
wide-expanding form (Grosv. No. 30), the dapper and gentle-

manly Colonel Nugent (Grosv. No. 136), painted in 1765,
and even the fine equestrian portrait of General Honeywood
(1765), must be passed without further reference.

The portrait of Lady Mary Bowlby (Grosv. No. 96), if
we mistake not, marks the transition to a more developed
style. Up to this time Gainsborough has shown himself
weak in the rendering of textures. He has tried his best, as
we have seen; but he has not been very successful. Hair
especially has eluded his grasp. We now find him steadily
advancing in this respect. The artistic qualities of his work
are becoming more pronounced. The picture is a pleasant
thing to look at, quite apart from the question of whether it
be a likeness or not. The colours work prettily together;
the light is well distributed. But, more than this, there is an
aspect of distinction infused into the subject. From the very
beginning Gainsborough had shared his own friendliness of
disposition with every person whose portrait he painted. He
had made them look forth for ever from his canvases with
welcoming and pleasant glances. Henceforward, whilst giving
further emphasis to this kindly quality, he made all his ladies,
at any rate, appear high-bred and distinguished, if they
were capable of so appearing. The power of imparting this
aspect of distinction is perhaps the special prerogative of
English artists. It was at all events a prerogative which
Reynolds and Gainsborough possessed to a remarkable degree.
The portrait of Lady Mary Bowlby is not a very conspicuous
example of its exercise, but it is important as an early example
in Gainsborough's case.

GAINSBOROUGH.

Mrs. Graham of Balgowan.

By an unhappy fatality it is almost impossible to talk about Gainsborough for very long without mentioning Reynolds, and sooner or later we shall have to ask whether either artist produced a visible effect upon the other. We know that the two men observed each other's work, as of course they could not fail to do. Gainsborough, looking at Reynolds' pictures, said, ' D—— him, how various he is !' and Reynolds, looking at Gainsborough's, declared, ' I cannot make out how he produces his effects ;' but both of these characteristic remarks were made at a later date than that to which we are now referring. Of course neither artist could help feeling the influence of the other to some extent, and the earliest instance I have been able to discover of Gainsborough's doing so is a half-length portrait of Mrs. Macauley (Grosv. No. 206), a picture not of much interest otherwise, but which appears to have been suggested by one of Reynolds's half-lengths of the type of Lady C. Keppel (Grosv. No. 123), painted in 1755. The influence is observable only in the pose ; all else is Gainsborough's own. Throughout life he kept his individuality pure from all extraneous matter. He nourished himself by observation, but he seldom imitated ; he assimilated. He studied, we may feel sure, whatever works of art, ancient or modern, came in his way. He copied pictures by Van Dyck, Titian, Rubens, and Teniers ; but, as Reynolds said of him, ' What he thus learned, he applied to the original of nature, which he saw with his own eyes ; and imitated, not in the manner of those masters, but in his own.'

IV.

THE famous portrait of Garrick (Grosv. No. 7) opens ·what
we may call Gainsborough's central Bath period, though, once
for all, it must be repeated that the development of Gainsborough's style does not naturally divide into periods; all lines
of division are arbitrary.   This picture was either bought by
the municipality of Stratford-upon-Avon or presented to them
by the great actor.   It shows him standing in a park, leaning
against a pedestal, with his arm round a bust of Shakspeare.
The position is easy and natural, the face is bright, the costume
pleasant in colour.   The trees, grass, and water of the background are painted in more detail than at a later time in the
artist's career they would have been ; nevertheless the landscape is treated as accessory to the figure, and so handled
rather in a decorative than a representative fashion.   When
Gainsborough's subject was landscape he worked in another
way, as we shall hereafter see.   He never combined a regular
landscape with a portrait.   The figures are either subservient
to the natural objects or the natural objects to the figures.
Sometimes, indeed, he introduced a likeness or two into his
landscapes, as, for instance, those of his daughters, in the
' Harvest Waggon ' (Grosv. Nos. 174 and 33), but then the
figures are mere sketches.   The landscape backgrounds of his
portraits take the place of decorative hangings.   They are
not intended to be looked at.   The beholder is meant to fix
his eye upon the person portrayed, and when he does so the
natural objects, vaguely suggested behind, take their proper

place. Regarded by themselves they do not satisfy the eye ; they do not retain hold upon it ; they send it back to the figure. As Gainsborough advanced in experience he more and more emphasised in his portraits this subordination of landscape to man.

He painted at least five portraits of Garrick, but the Stratford full-length is the most famous. His admiration for the actor is well known. To Henderson he wrote, ' Stick to Garrick as close as you can, for your life : you should follow his heels like his shadow in sunshine. . . . . . Garrick is the greatest creature living, in every respect ; he is worth studying in every action. Every view, and every idea of him, is worthy of being stored up for imitation ; and I have ever found him a generous and a sincere friend. Look upon him, Henderson, with your imitative eyes, for when he drops you'll have nothing but poor old Nature's book to look in. You'll be left to grope about alone, scratching your pate in the dark, or by a farthing candle. Now is your time, my lively fellow !' There is a letter of the year 1772 from Gainsborough to Garrick, referring to a portrait of the actor for which the artist was not going to allow him to pay. ' It was to be my present to Mrs. Garrick, and so it shall be in spite of your blood. . . . . I know your great stomach, that you hate to be crammed, but you shall swallow this one bait. . . God bless all your endeavours to delight the world, and may you sparkle to the last !'

Anyone's endeavours to delight the world were sure to call down at any rate Gainsborough's blessings. Actors and musicians were his brothers. Young Henderson came to

Bath, and Gainsborough took him to his heart at once, and
when he left for London followed him with letters of good
advice. 'Do but recollect how many hard-featured fellows
there are in the world that frown in the midst of enjoyment,
chew with unthankfulness, and seem to swallow with pain
instead of pleasure ; now anyone who sees you eat pig and
plum-sauce, immediately feels that pleasure which a plump
morsel, smoothly gliding through a narrow glib passage
into the regions of bliss, and moistened with the dews of
imagination, naturally creates. Some iron-faced dogs, you
know, seem to chew dry ingratitude, and swallow discontent.
Let such be kept to *under parts,* and never trusted to support
a character. In all but eating, stick to Garrick ; in *that* let
him stick to you, for I'll be curst if you are not his master !
Never mind the fools who talk of imitation and copying ; all
is imitation. . . . . What makes the difference, between man
and man, is real performance, and not genius or conception.
There are a thousand Garricks, a thousand Giardinis, and
Fischers, and Abels. Why only one Garrick with Garrick's
eyes, voice, etc. ? One Giardini with Giardini's fingers, etc. ?
But one Fischer with Fischer's dexterity, quickness, etc. ? Or,
more than one Abel with Abel's feeling upon the instrument ?
All the rest of the world are mere *hearers* and *see'rs.*'

At Bath Gainsborough lived amongst these light-hearted
companions, and painted portraits of them all. He painted
Henderson two or three times,* Abel he painted twice,

* A bust portrait at the Grosvenor Exhibition (No. 142) was christened
Henderson, though it was not stated on what grounds the attribution was made.

Giardini once, Fischer once, besides many more. The three-quarter length of Abel (Grosv. No. 46) with his *viol-di-gamba* between his knees, has now lost much of its charm of colour, but remains a solid piece of work. The full-length of Fischer (Grosv. No. 112) painted in 1767, is one of the best productions of this part of Gainsborough's life. The musician leans upon a pianoforte, with music-books, a hautboy, and a violin lying about. His pose is excellent in its naturalness; his face is very thoroughly painted. The man is pausing in the act of composition, and looking upwards with the bright glance of friendly intelligence, which none but Gainsborough could depict so well. Of all the artist's pictures, this is the one in which the accessories are most numerous and painted with most care and finish; for Gainsborough loved musical instruments almost as much as he loved musicians. He was no mean performer himself, and Jackson declared that 'there were times when music seemed to be Gainsborough's employment and painting his diversion.'

'When I first knew Gainsborough,' he says, 'he lived at Bath, where Giardini had been exhibiting his then unrivalled powers on the violin. His excellent performance made the painter enamoured of that instrument, and he was not satisfied until he possessed it. He next heard Abel on the *viol-di-gamba*. The violin was hung on the willow—Abel's viol-de-gamba was purchased, and the house resounded with melodious thirds and fifths. My friend's passion had now a fresh object—Fischer's hautboy; but I do not recollect that he deprived Fischer of his instrument, and although he procured a hautboy, I never heard him make the least attempt on it.   The next time I saw Gainsborough it was in the character of King David.   He had heard a harper at Bath—the performer was soon left harpless; and now Fischer, Abel, and Giardini were all forgotten—there was nothing like chords and arpeggios!

'Happening on a time to see a theorbo in a picture of Van Dyck's, Gainsborough concluded because, perhaps, it was finely painted, that the theorbo must be a fine instrument.   He recollected to have heard of a German professor, and ascending to his garret found him dining on roasted apples, and smoking his pipe with his theorbo beside him.

'"I am come to buy your lute.   Name your price, and here's your money."

'"I cannot sell my lute."

'"No! not for a guinea or two?   But you must sell it, I tell you!"

'"My lute is worth much money.   It is worth ten guineas."

'"Aye! that is it.   See; here's the money!"   So saying he took up the instrument, laid down the price, went half-way down the stair, and returned.

'"I have done but half my errand; what is your lute worth if I have not your book?"

'"What book, Master Gainsborough?"

'"Why, the book of airs you have composed for the lute."

' " Ah, sir, I can never part with my book !"

' " Poh ! you can make another at any time. This is the book I mean—there's ten guineas for it—so once more good day." He went down a few steps, and returned again.

' " What use is your book to me if I don't understand it ? And your lute, you may take it again if you won't teach me to play on it. Come home with me, and give me the first lesson."

' " I will come to-morrow."

' " You must come now."

' " I must dress myself."

' " For what ? You are the best figure I have seen to-day."

' " I must shave, sir."

' " I honour your beard."

' " I must, however, put on my wig."

' " D—— your wig ! your cap and beard become you ! Do you think if Van Dyck was to paint you he'd let you be shaved ?" '

All his life long, indeed, music had the most powerful fascination for Gainsborough, and it is related of him and Fischer that ' the two enthusiasts sometimes left their spouses to sleep away more than half the night alone. For one would get at his flageolet, which he played delightfully, and the other at his *viol-di-gamba*, and have such an inveterate set-to, that, as Mrs. Gainsborough said, a gang of robbers might have stripped the house and set it on fire, to boot, and the gentlemen been never the wiser.'

V.

It would be a mistake to conclude that anything of this seeming inconstancy of disposition was reflected in Gainsborough's art; he was not a man to be continually trying experiments and changing his style. Throughout the whole of the Bath period he steadily advanced in power along one line. The portraits painted by him between the years 1765 and 1770 are all solid pieces of work; dashing traces of genius are less visible in them than the careful results of labour. The half-length of Mr. Amyand (Grosv. No. 141) is a good example of the period. It is a picture one might pass over many times, yet once it has attracted the attention it keeps hold of it. There is a sly under-current of good humour in the expression which is rendered with remarkable subtlety, not by any lucky strokes of the brush, but by a careful modelling of all the features. Subtleties . of expression now become more and more common. A look of suppressed truculence distinguishes Mr. Almack (Grosv. No. 64), a wild thoughtlessness animates the glance and pose of Lady Margaret Lindsay (Grosv. No. 160), whilst the kindly and benevolent soul of John Thornton (Grosv. No. 36) can even be discerned beneath his fat and almost piggish countenance. But it is the three-quarter-length portrait of the third Duke of Buccleuch (Grosv. No. 66) that gives clearest proof of the skill which Gainsborough had now acquired. The living man, with his arms round a pet dog, smiles at you out of the canvas

with peculiar vividness; the flesh quivers about the start-
lingly bright eyes. Gainsborough at this time always made
his figures active. You do not look at them, it is they that
regard you. The spectator is passive, the picture active.
In a room full of Gainsborough's portraits, the beholder is
a hundred times beheld; he stands surrounded by a 'crowd
of witnesses,' who are not there to be looked at but themselves to look.

Few pictures are more remarkable in this respect than
the half-length portrait of the famous Lord Chesterfield
(Grosv. No. 84), painted in 1769. The man is there,
hidden behind his 'impenetrable mask' of a countenance,
and with his head buried in an old-fashioned wig. His eye
regards you with steely-cold observation. On the whole,
he does not seem to think much of you. He is very old,
has lost all his front teeth, and the weight of his eyelids
is almost too much for his strength; but he is far from
considering himself a show, he is a critic, and he takes the
measure, so it seems, of one after another of those filing
before him, who falsely deem themselves spectators.

From a distance the half-length of Mr. R. Palmer
(Grosv. No. 210), with the twinkling eyes and the face
running over with expression, seems a most elaborately
finished work, but when you regard the canvas closely
this effect is found to be an illusion. Every touch has
been applied with that definite knowledge of the end it
was to produce, which henceforward became Gainsborough's
peculiar prerogative. The same thing can be noticed in

the half-lengths of the Duchess of Montague (Grosv. No. 28) and the Duke of Bedford (Grosv. No. 38), both painted in or about the year 1768. We can trace in these three pictures the earliest clear foreshadowing of the painter's final style. The effect seems to be attained by magic. What, beheld close, looks like a mere tissue of fine lines of different colours, laid in all manner of directions as though by mere caprice, takes on, when surveyed from a short distance, the aspect of most finished work. The artist's conception and mode of expression became henceforward so intimately connected, that no severance is possible between them. From this time his style was fixed. It was to this final style that Reynolds referred when he said, ‘It is certain that all those odd scratches and marks which, on a close examination, are so observable in Gainsborough's pictures, and which even to experienced painters appear rather the effect of accident than design—this chaos, this uncouth and shapeless appearance, by a kind of magic, at a certain distance assumes form, and all the parts seem to drop into their proper places, so that we can hardly refuse acknowledging the full effect of diligence, under the appearance of chance and hasty negligence. That Gainsborough himself considered this peculiarity in his manner and the power it possesses of exciting surprise as a beauty in his works, I think may be inferred from the eager desire which we know he always expressed, that his pictures at the exhibition should be seen near as well as at a distance.’

GAINSBOROUGH.

Admiral Lord Rodney.

Already, in a letter written from Ipswich in the year
1758, Gainsborough had foreshadowed the tendency of his
style. 'You please me much,' he said, 'by saying that no
other fault is found in your picture than the roughness of the
surface ; for that part being of use in giving force to the effect
at a proper distance, and what a judge of painting knows an
original from a copy by—in short, being the touch of the
pencil which is harder to preserve than smoothness. I am
much better pleased that they should spy out things of that
kind, than to see an eye half an inch out of its place, or a
nose out of drawing when viewed at a proper distance. I
don't think it would be more ridiculous for a person to put
his nose close to the canvas, and say the colours smelt offen-
sive, than to say how rough the paint lies ; for one is just as
material as the other with regard to hurting the effect and
drawing of a picture.'

Let the year 1768, then, be remembered in connexion
with Gainsborough, as that in which his final style declared
itself. The portrait of the Duke of Bedford (died 1771)
is an example of that style in almost complete development ;
but it stands alone in this respect, and may possibly have
been painted by the artist some years later from a sketch
made about this time. It is not until 1780 that Gainsborough's hatching manner reached its full development,
and perhaps led him a little astray.

Some of his best pictures belong to the period inter-
vening between 1770 and 1780. Foremost amongst these
is the full-length portrait of Jonathan Buttal, world-renowned

as the 'Blue Boy' (Grosv. No. 62). It is probably the 'Portrait of a Young Gentleman,' the 'Portrait of a Gentleman in a Van Dyck Habit,' exhibited by Gainsborough at the Royal Academy in 1770. At all events, to judge from internal evidence, the picture was painted about that year, and not in 1779, as many writers have affirmed. It is a matter for great regret that, since the time when the picture was last exhibited, it should have seriously deteriorated, whether owing to injudicious treatment or from some unavoidable cause. Nevertheless it remains a masterpiece of art, and by it alone Gainsborough might consent to be judged. The lad is represented clothed in a blue silk coat and breeches, and standing bare-headed upon the ground in the open air. His plumed hat is held in his right hand; behind him is a richly-coloured background of dark landscape and lurid sky. The edges of the many folds of his silk garments are illuminated, and between them rifts of warm brown shadow break up the blue masses of light and, with the help of the background, give a rich tone to the whole. It is a mistake to consider that the picture was painted as a refutation of Reynolds's dictum, 'that the masses of light in a picture' should be 'always of a warm, mellow colour—yellow, red, or a yellowish-white; and that the blue, the gray, or the green colours, be kept almost entirely out of these masses, and be used only to support and set off these warm colours, and for this purpose a small proportion of cold colours will be sufficient. Let this conduct be reversed—let the light be cold and the surrounding colours warm, as we often see in the works of the Roman and Florentine painters, and it will be out of the power of art, even in the hands of Rubens or Titian, to make a picture splendid and harmonious.' The discourse in which this passage occurs was not delivered till 1778, and the picture, as we have said, is in the style of many years before. The attitude of the lad is, to all intents, the same as that of young Lord Powis in the early picture above described. In one of the last, if not the very last picture finished by Gainsborough, the full-length portrait of the Duke of Norfolk (Grosv. No. 253), the same attitude and the same style of costume again recur; but the scheme of light and colour was different, and the work by no means so fine.

The 'Blue Boy' is, of all Gainsborough's pictures, that in which genius, labour, and developed skill, meet in most balanced harmony. The works of his earlier days are marked by great painstaking and steady increase in power; but they always lack the full artistic grasp of the subject which the painter here and henceforward attains. On the other hand, the works of the last decade of Gainsborough's life are lacking in due elaboration. They are often little more than very clever sketches. In the 'Blue Boy' we behold a fine conception cleverly, skilfully, and carefully worked out. The face is full of life and sweet attractiveness, and is, at the same time, thoroughly modelled. The lights and shadows show bolder contrasts and work together to a more noble unity, than in any earlier picture. The

F

chord of colour is rich and mellow. Every detail of work, from end to end of the canvas, is marshalled like the units in a well-ordered host, and directed towards the end in view.

Curiously enough, the conception of this — the most solid and laboured of Gainsborough's mature works—is, for him, of an exceptional character. The lad does not stand in the sunshine of life, but in a mysterious and almost fiery gloom. His face lacks the young brightness and friendliness of expression that almost all the artist's full-grown sitters were caused to manifest. The picture is, however, an exception only in so far as it belongs to an exceptional class. Let the reader cast his eye in recollection over all the pictures of children painted by Gainsborough in his maturity—the 'Cottage Girl' (Grosv. No. 173); the 'Wood-gatherers' (Grosv. No. 82); the 'Milk Girl' (Grosv. No. 49); and even the sketches of 'Jack Hill' (Grosv. Nos. 86 and 95) —he will find that in all of them the child's expression is plaintive, almost to the verge of sadness. Grown men and women, who might be supposed by this time to know the hollowness of life—some Lady Margaret Fordyce, for instance, dancing the long night through on the ruins of her husband's reputation—nothing but laughter and the aspect of joy was grim enough for them. But the artist could not look upon the innocent ignorance of childhood without a pang; and he unconsciously transferred to the object of his tender regret the feeling which was personal to himself. Many times and oft, we doubt not, Gainsborough's merry mood thatched out for him a yawning abyss of midnight

GAINSBOROUGH.

Cottage Children and Landscape.

storm, the muffled roar of which he heard through all his
laughter.

The pathetic aspect of life is sometimes more manifest to
the seemingly joyous than to those for whom sadness is a
profession. One of the last stories told of Gainsborough
bears this out. Sir George Beaumont, Sheridan, and the
painter were dining together, but Gainsborough sat in un-
wonted silence, 'with a look of fixed melancholy which no
wit could dissipate. At length he took Sheridan by the
hand, led him out of the room, and said, "Now, don't
laugh, but listen. I shall die soon—I know it—I feel it
—I have less time to live than my looks infer ; but for
this I care not. What oppresses my mind is this : I have
many acquaintances and few friends ; and as I wish to
have one worthy man to accompany me to the grave, I
am desirous of bespeaking you. Will you come—aye or
no ?"' Sheridan promised, and Gainsborough became himself again. 'Throughout the rest of the evening his wit
flowed, and his humour ran over ; and the minutes, like
those of the poet, winged their way with pleasure.'

The 'Blue Boy' is, of all Gainsborough's pictures, that
wherein he most closely follows the footsteps of Van Dyck.
Gainsborough was not an imitator, though he was always
an earnest student of other men's works. It is only, therefore, occasionally, and then by chance, that we can point
to one of his pictures, and say, 'This is the result of Van
Dyck's influence, this of Titian's.' There are, however,
two more portraits painted about this time, in which Gains-

borough followed Van Dyck almost as closely as he does
in the 'Blue Boy.' They are the bust portrait of Lord
Bateman (Grosv. No. 5) and the charming unfinished head
of Gainsborough Dupont (Grosv. No. 146), which was
perhaps painted a little later. The beautiful little half-
length of Edward Gardiner (Grosv. No. 132), made about
the year 1780, must be grouped with these ; and the three
together form the brightest, freshest, and most charming
of all the artist's portraits of young persons.

VI.

In the summer of 1774 Gainsborough wisely moved to
London, and Schomberg House became his home for the
remaining fourteen years of his life. He was soon sum-
moned to the royal palace, and he shared with West the
patronage of the Court. During the first four or five
years of his London period, his work was done with ease,
and yet also with care and application. He increased in
power and skill, and was thereby enabled to work faster
than before. Commissions streamed in upon him ; he was
in every sense a successful man. To this period belongs
the portrait rendered famous by its mysterious disappearance.
It was believed to represent the Duchess of Devonshire ;
but the face and figure did not resemble hers, as a comparison of engravings clearly shows.*

The half-length portraits of Ladies Erne and Dillon

* It was Mr. Scharf who pointed out this fact to me.

(Old Masters, 1885, No. 17), painted in 1776, and the fine half-length of Mr. Christie (Grosv. No. 67), painted two years later, are solid and characteristic works of this period. The half-length portrait of himself (Grosv. No. 185), and the beautiful full-face picture of Mrs. Gainsborough in a black mantilla, both belong to about this time; whilst the full-length group of their daughters (Grosv. No. 91) cannot have come much later. The last-mentioned picture is worth dwelling upon for a moment. The two young ladies, dressed in all their finery, are standing with their dog in front of a wooded landscape, which for varied light and colour is one of the most pleasing of the painter's backgrounds. The costumes are elaborately painted, and the textures of their several parts are skilfully rendered. As usual with Gainsborough's sitters, the ladies have a light, transparent scarf about them for variety's sake. The artist has done his best to make them look dignified and high-bred. His truthful eye, however, has forbidden him to see falsely; and notwithstanding the pose which he has been willing to lend them their faces contradict the intended effect. The picture looks laboured and put together; it wants spontaneity. Mrs. Gainsborough in her chair is a far finer work, for she is her own natural self acting no part. Better also are the half-length portraits of the girls painted a few years later. Their father then took them as he found them: Mary, who ran away with Fischer in 1780, leaning back playing a guitar, and Margaret in a perfectly rendered green costume and hat, seated upright in the open air.

Both the last-mentioned pictures are examples of the work of Gainsborough's last years, to which we must now briefly refer. From the beginning, as we have seen, he aimed at making every part of his picture tend towards the single intention of the whole. For a long time this was but an aim. In his central period success began to attend his efforts. At last, from about 1780 onwards, this quality became the finest characteristic of all his works. It is now clear that, as Reynolds says, he formed 'all the parts of his picture together; the whole going on at the same time, in the same manner as Nature creates her works.' When once he had conceived his subject, he painted it with lightning-like speed. He did not merely conceive the head or the figure, and then paint in suitable accessories. In his mind he saw the picture entire from end to end, and he caused it to take visible form, working at the whole of it at once. Owing to the very crispness of his impressions, he was led to work more and more slightly; lest in the realisation the spirit of the conception should vanish. He was 'a man of strong intuitive perception of what was required.' He knew what he set out to effect; and when he had attained that he ceased, and cared not whether in other respects his picture seemed unfinished. Do not regard the details of Gainsborough's later works, but look at the whole as he conceived the whole, and you will find that the expressional power of the man was little less than perfect. The conception we can often afford to criticise, but the expression, in these last years, never. 'The slightness,' says

Reynolds, 'which we see in his best works cannot always be imputed to negligence. However they may appear to superficial observers, painters know very well that a steady attention to the general effect takes up more time, and is much more laborious to the mind, than any mode of high finishing or smoothness without such attention. . . . Gainsborough's portraits were often little more, in regard to finishing or determining the form of the features, than what generally attends a dead colour ; but as he was always attentive to the general effect, or whole together, I have often imagined that this unfinished manner contributed even to that striking resemblance for which his portraits are so remarkable.'

Take, as examples of the work of this final period, such pictures as the portraits of the Prince of Wales ('Old Masters,' 1884, No. 151), and Colonel St. Leger (Grosv. No. 23), or the Mrs. Siddons (National Gallery), or the Duchess of Devonshire (Grosv. No. 145), or Mr. and Mrs. Hallett ('Old Masters,' 1885, No. 195), or Sir Henry and Lady Bate Dudley (Grosv. Nos. 171 and 75). The artist's conception in every one of these cases, besides being a genuinely artistic one, is expressed with a precision beyond praise. The duskiness of the backgrounds, the glossiness of silk, the fluffiness of feathers and trimmings, are all used, not for their own sakes, or as charming separately by themselves, but as indivisibly component parts in a single whole. It is this working together of all things to one end that raises Gainsborough to such a height among artists. For the power of effecting this is the great and essential quality

that makes a man an artist. Gainsborough never forgets
that paint is his language and the brush his instrument of
expression. He does not lay on his colours in the manner
of an engraver, as Dürer did, or in any other manner except
that which is right to a painter and to no other. He thought
in paint, so to speak, and saw everything from the point of
view of the brush. He sought first for charms of colour ;
by aid of colour he said what he had to say. As the years
went by he was more and more content to suggest an impression of brightness and harmonious tint rather than to
give full realisation to an appearance.

The wonderful half-lengths of young George Canning
(Grosv. No. 100), Lady Mulgrave ('Old Masters,' 1885,
No. 47), and Mrs. Fitzherbert (Grosv. No. 10), are excellent examples of this. The last-mentioned is one of the
slightest and most vivid of Gainsborough's works. The
least of its merits is that it catches the haughty, smiling
expression of the sitter with more than the accuracy of an
instantaneous photograph. But the lady's character is not
alone shown in her face and posture, nor even in the design
of her garments. The impression the sight of her produced
upon the artist has thrilled through him in all the work, and
has been one of the guiding forces that directed his hand ;
so that every track of the brush is instinct with the same
spirit that animates the whole conception. Look closely at
the canvas, and the costume resolves itself into a writhing
mass of soft, streaky, ribbon-like brush-tracks, curled and
twirled about in a wondrous seeming confusion, yet in reality

GAINSBOROUGH.

Georgiana, Duchess of Devonshire.

held together by an unfailing law, and directed with faultless certainty to a definite effect. Stand at the intended distance, and the whole unites into a perfect harmony. Zig-zag lines resolve themselves into the semblance of stuffs, and render the intended form, colour, and texture, as by a magical power. Those parts of the canvas scarcely touched by colour are not noticed. The frame becomes a window. Through it you behold the lady at a chosen moment, amidst chosen surroundings, in a chosen posture, and you behold her, not with your own eyes, but through the eyes of a man trained and skilled to look aright.

VII.

WE have thus passed in rapid review the stages of Gainsborough's development as portrait-painter. His landscape shall now be the subject of a briefer and more hesitating sketch. It is our misfortune that the artist never signed or dated any of his landscapes, and only one or two of his portraits. Not only so, but the exhibition catalogues do not help us, for though we know that Gainsborough exhibited three on this occasion, five on the other, and so forth, we can seldom identify them. He left no diary or note-book to supply the defect of other chronological data. In fact, he was an artist, pure and simple; the creation of pictures was fact enough for him, and all he asked of men was that they should look at them and find pleasure in them, not that they should arrange them in chronological order. Times are changed now, and the historical spirit, for better or worse, has got us in its grasp. Pictures, like all other things, must take their places as links in the endless chain of development, that holds us anchored over the unmeasured depths of the ocean of the past.

Landscape had peculiar charm for Gainsborough from his earliest years. It was his boyish instinct to wander forth into the woods and fields of his native country to feast his eyes upon the fair sights of nature. In school and out of school his pencil was always at work, surreptitiously or otherwise. He had no one to teach him except his mother, who is known to have possessed some skill with her brush ; but he went forward blindly under the compelling force of an innate tendency. His boyish efforts are said to have shown no particular merit. The promise lay not in any early performance, but in the instinct that fixed the lad's energies in one unvarying direction. Landscape-painting was not then an English art. Its only recognised use was as background for portrait, and even so it was employed but sparingly.

When Gainsborough was a student in London there was nothing to attract him to cultivate landscape-painting. Portraiture was alone in demand. If amateurs wanted landscapes they bought the works of the Low-Country painters of the preceding century. A few people wished to have pictures made of their country-seats, but this kind of work was ill paid, and a low level of art was all that such productions required, or indeed gave scope for. Wilson, who was thirteen years older than Gainsborough, starved all his life as a landscape-painter.

An artist who wished to make landscape his subject had to find some other means for his support. It is thus obvious that Gainsborough could have had no teaching, worthy of the name, in this branch of art. His early landscapes are only rapid transcripts of impressions made upon him by particular scenes. They have little charm of colour or light, and are lacking in all idea of composition. The young artist had no notion of making a unity out of the infinity that lay before him. The story of the growth of that notion in his mind is the history of his development as a landscape artist.

His masters in landscape-painting were the pictures of his Dutch and Flemish forerunners. These he saw and sometimes copied in the houses of country gentlemen, to which he had access after leaving London and settling as portrait-painter in Suffolk. Sometimes we find him under the influence of one man, sometimes of another. He imitated Hobbema, Du Jardin, Ruysdael, Rubens, Wynants, Gaspar Poussin, Claude, and Cuyp, one after another. His development as a landscape-painter was much more irregular than his development as a painter of portraits. He had no Hayman to help him lay the foundations of a style of his own. He had to grope a way for himself, and in his search he went now in one direction, now in another. Most of his early landscapes suggest the style of a known master. One landscape (Grosv. No. 24), with a distant dome of rain-cloud projected against a light blue sky, tells of the influence of Du Jardin ; whilst another (Grosv. No. 15), in which a road passes by a clump of trees in the foreground, and then winds away to a distance of low, undulating country, under a sky decked with soft, rounded clouds, part sun-lit, part in shadow, recalls Hobbema in the general brownness of its tones. In this way we can often trace portions of the rising artist's path-way of advance, but we have little or nothing to help us in joining these portions together. We cannot tell which is first, and which follows. One thing, however, is clear, that, as in portraiture, so eventually also in landscape, what Gains-borough learned from others 'he applied to the originals of nature, which he saw with his own eyes ; and imitated, not in the manner of other artists, but in his own.'

Stronger than any other influence upon him was the influence of that Suffolk landscape in the midst of which his boyhood's hours were passed. He looked at Nature, wher-ever he was, through Suffolk-trained eyes. The gently-rolling country, with its wide-backed fields, its lanes, its small woods, its scattered trees along the hedge-rows ; the mounting clouds piled up on high, and nursing storm within their depths, such clouds as in the summer-time come majestically down the valleys of Orwell and Stour, the sudden views of well-farmed country, seen round a corner of trees at the turn of a road—these and the like are subjects of unfailing charm to him. He finds about Bath or Richmond, or wherever he may be, sights that awaken the happy memories of his Suffolk days, and those memories always infuse themselves into his work.

One quality Gainsborough's early landscapes possess in common with his portraits of the same period : they are painted with care in a detailed fashion. There is no attempt to catch effects by lucky hits. Everything that is attained is attained by labour and definite intention. He did not choose a great variety of subjects at this time ; he contented himself with simple scenes, and treated them in a simple style. Some old lichen-covered tree-trunk lies or leans in the foreground, with the sun-light playing on the sharp edges of its riven bark. Large-leaved docks flourish at its foot, and a stretch of brown grass, brightly illuminated, carries the eye back to a shadowed middle distance. Perhaps there is a ford with cattle crossing it in the foreground, or, mayhap, brown banks, capped with dark green carpets of grass, shut in a narrow lane, along which pack-horses tread their leisurely way. Once, indeed, we have a landscape (Grosv. No. 51) whence the very memory of animal life seems to be banished. There is not a house in sight. No bird flutters in the air, no beast grazes or sleeps in the field. A sky, wherein there are at any rate some patches of pure blue, looks down upon all the prospects of this period. Massed squadrons of cumuli usually march along the horizon, beating back the sunlight from their bright crests and nurturing gloom in their bosoms. In early attempts these clouds are sharply outlined and crisply modelled, but presently they become shrouded in a tender mist, softening their edges and involving them and the distant country in a common mystery. They are fair-weather clouds at first, and suggest rather the memory than the prophecy of storm.

But, still in early years, this is changed, and Gainsborough begins to paint visions seen under the last bright rays of a sun about to be hidden. We must rejoice and

take pleasure while we may. The nearest cottage will
soon be our refuge. 'The night cometh when no man can
work,' and the rain under which none can delight. The
rolling cumulus climbs into the sky and nods its threatening
head. It marches no longer across the horizon, but comes
steadily over the wide meadows towards us. One landscape
(Grosv. No. 133) is an excellent example of this favourite
subject, the threatening storm-cloud. A man and a pair of
feeble horses are ploughing in the brown foreground ; behind
them a brown bank leans against a knoll, crowned with a
dark windmill. Farther back is a slowly-rising slope, draped
with fields, and over all a portentous, bulging cloud towers
brilliantly into the air, trailing a skirt of darkness behind it.

Gainsborough never found in a windmill the many moods
that his fellow-countyman, John Constable, discovered in it.
He could not altogether overlook the patient creature; but
when it appears in his pictures, it usually stands sentinel on
the brow of some distant eminence. It does so, for instance,
in a charming landscape (Grosv. No. 157) prophetic of
Linnell, where a farm-house looks forth amongst trees from
beyond a river at the foot of a church-crowned hill. All
this, however, is but subordinate to the inevitable trunk in
the foreground, with peasants and cows at its foot. A mere
glance at any collection of Gainsborough's early landscapes
shows the charm which the trunk of a full-grown tree
possessed for him. He painted some pictures for the sake
of a monumental stem planted in the foreground, and once
(Grosv. No. 18) that was the only part he finished ; for when

GAINSBOROUGH.

Landscape near Sudbury, Suffolk ; the Artist's birthplace.

he had played with its rusty forms, and lingered affectionately over every detail of its scarred surface, he laid the canvas aside, having no interest to spare for the remainder. In this picture, and in another (Grosv. No. 202) of similar type — careless gipsies gathered about a fire for their evening meal, and an ass, patient and picturesque, are the well-chosen companions of the old dryad of the forest. The group clusters on the brow of a hill, whence the eye wanders across indistinct, cultivated country, bathed in twilight, to the cloud-fretting beams of the setting sun.

All these pictures give more or less evidence of minute study of the details of nature. Trees seem to be painted leaf by leaf. Plants in the foreground are rendered with studious insight into individual form. Nothing is ignorantly or unintentionally omitted. Nothing is wilfully slurred over. One of the most ambitious and important landscapes of this period (Old Masters, 1885, No. 71) renders a view from the outskirts of a wood looking towards a gently rippling country of field and farmstead. Scattered outposts of big trees arise on either hand, low underwood lurks in the shadow beneath, and an undisciplined path wanders down towards the meadows. There the sunlight lies abroad on grass and hedgerow, roof and village tower. All beyond is neat and trim in contrast to the pathetic negligence of the broken foreground, whose only inhabitant, a footsore wayfarer, sits pitying his weary limbs. Every part of this picture is painted with great detail. The fields and buildings of the distance are little less minutely wrought than the foliage of the foreground. The very blades of grass in front seem to be individually painted. Nevertheless, this picture, in common with most of its fellows of the same period, labours under one defect—it lacks the highest kind of unity. The artist has not impressed a scene upon his mind as a whole, before setting to work to realise it upon his canvas. He has transcribed instead of creating. He has taken his details one by one from nature, and one by one fitted them together. He has caught a series of scattered suggestions instead of a single rounded idea. Full daylight may, for example, be strewn over the foreground whilst a sunset is lingering on the distant horizon; or the sky may be suggestive of wind, and the foliage of repose. The landscape is not the expression of a single conception. It is interesting to watch the endeavours of the painter to remedy this defect. In a small and relatively early picture (Grosv. No. 73), the attempt has been made to bring the sunset into the foreground as well as into the distance; but it has not succeeded. A little view (Grosv. No. 106) of an old stone bridge crossed by a caravan of pack-horses is far better. Here wind is the unifying factor. The beasts plod patiently along with their heads down; the riders submit to discomfort, resistance being useless. Clouds hurry across the sky; the trees bend to the blast; and a few spare leaves shiver on an old trunk in the foreground. The whole is painted in a freer fashion than before. Details are suggested rather than depicted. Nevertheless, the work is really finer. Unity—the essence of landscape art—is attained.

VIII.

THE pictures we have now to consider were painted during the latter half of Gainsborough's period of residence at Bath. He felt himself upon firmer ground than before. His aims were becoming more precise. His work, therefore, was done with less hesitation. The end being clearly in view, the steps to be taken to reach it were likewise more clearly perceived. Thus he painted in a bolder style, and naturally also on a larger scale. A woodland glade (Grosv. No. 124) may be taken as example of the work of the transition period. The foreground is occupied by some rather idealised peasants, with their cows, goats, and sheep resting by the way. Behind them is a row of trees. There is a glimpse of wider country beyond, with a church tower peering forth in the midst. The foliage is of a rather tufty or feathery character—a kind which in Gainsborough's later work becomes unpleasantly common. But we have selected this picture for special notice because of the sky, which wears a hazy blue tint, except where the sunlight whitens the clouds. The light does not merely rest upon them; it pours everywhere like a flood and mellows all objects. It is an unnatural seeming light, reminiscent of sunsets on canvas rather than in the heavens. It is not Gainsborough's spontaneous idea. It did not arise from contemplation of an actual scene, but from study of Gaspar Poussin's pictures or Claude's. Gainsborough is, for once, a confessed imitator. His idealised peasants are open admission of the fact; and, to make the state of things more evident, there are a pair of fighting dogs right in front, borrowed unblushingly from Snyders.

The ' Harvest Waggon' (Grosv. No. 33) is a finer and more independent work. Here Gainsborough shows himself a free man, able to regard things from a wider-reaching point of view entirely his own. He planned the picture with care, as his preliminary sketch (Grosv. No. 174) sufficiently proves. The composition is simple. There is a wood on one side, and the other a pond, with a few trees beyond it. A road passes on between the wood and the pond ; and the waggon, drawn by a picturesque team of horses, halts for a moment in the middle of the view to allow one of Gainsborough's daughters, disguised as a peasant maiden, to climb in and join her sister and friends. There is a vista of flat country in the distance, and the sky is full of piled masses of sunlit cloud. The whole is, as it were, flung down in living unity. The delicate grace of natural forms is sacrificed to a strong general effect. Thus the sombre appearance of a mass of shadowed foliage is obtained, though not the lightness of rustling leaves. The glossy surface of water is there, but we miss its subtle transparencies and mystery of ripple-crossed reflexions. The lean and bony horses are of a raggedly picturesque character, harmonising with the spirit of the whole work ; but they are only sketched in with a few pregnant strokes. It is in Gainsborough's equestrian portraits alone that he seems to have cared about painting a finely bred horse for the sake of its grace of form and glossiness of coat. Little choice, indeed, was there left him in the matter. When, as in his landscapes, he could do what he pleased, he chose ragged and picturesque animals, old and tired, or at any rate bony and uncouth. The leader of the team in the 'Harvest Waggon' was presented to Gainsborough by Wiltshire, the Bath carrier, who used to convey the artist's pictures to London free of charge, for admiration's sake. The beast is anxious to go on towards home, so the carter at his head has just startled him back by a rap on the nose, and the painter has caught him on the instant in this sudden attitude, with his head thrown up and his mane jerked loose in the air. The whole is similarly the result of a single impression, and each part is finished far enough to suggest that impression and no more. Gainsborough gave this picture to Wiltshire, and in giving it he stated that it pleased him 'more than any he had ever executed.' We can well believe this to have been so, for the mode of conception and style of execution seen in the 'Harvest Waggon' were adhered to by the artist with increasing success during the remainder of his life as a landscape-painter.

Henceforward we have but to mark the stages of a continuous advance. The landscape painted at Shockerwick (Grosv. No. 54) is a notable work, telling of the continued influence of Claude and Gaspar Poussin. The beholder looks down a little valley shut in by rocks and trees on either hand. The stream, arrested upon a rocky step, forms a pool in the foreground; and there three cows are halting on their homeward way whilst the milkmaid receives the

attentions of her lover under the shadow of a neighbouring
rock.   The valley trends westward, and grants a view over
wide country and away to the golden sky.   The sunset-light
penetrates everywhere, and gives a character to everything.
It touches the trees and gilds the backs of the kine ; it warms
the clouds ; it comes up from the pool ; it permeates the
atmosphere.   The foliage is painted in Gainsborough's best
mood.   It is variegated in texture and colour, besides being
light and transparent.   ˙Everything is swiftly and skilfully
suggested.   Doubtless, if the unity of the conception had
been maintained, and, at the same time, details had been
rendered with more loving care, the picture would have been
a finer work.   But the essential thing in landscape-art is
there.   The picture is not a transcript of a locality ; it is the
suggestion of the impression made upon an impressionable
person by the sight of a beautiful view seen under favourable
circumstances of weather, light, and colour.   Equally suggestive, but no more complete, is the view in Shropshire
(Grosv. No. 129).   We are again made to look along a
westward-trending valley towards a golden nebula of light
condensed in a clear evening sky.   Trees reach themselves
across the sunset, and a brook flows forward under a rock,
and then bends round and passes out of sight.

Clearly, Gainsborough's sympathies were only evoked by
a limited range of landscape subjects.   It is needless to look
to him for the wild and weird aspects of nature.   He is the
painter of pastoral scenes, beheld usually under one of two
aspects.   Either the sky is full of clouds, threatening rain,

and the wind is blowing, or about to blow, or else the air
is full of peace and the setting sun casts its slanting rays
across tilth, meadow, and woodland. The landscape in
Herefordshire (Grosv. No. 68) is scarcely an exception to
this rule. It is, indeed, entitled 'Going to Market;' but the
peasants with their horses laden with vegetables seem rather
to be returning from their labours in the fields than starting
out for a day's business. The sky, moreover, is full of a
soft light, which might be the light of dawn, were it not that
the horses do not step with the freshness of morning, but
plod along as though weary after a day's hard work. Once
again rich foliaged trees, hastily sketched in, project themselves against the sky, the artist finding in their domed tops
something of the quality which rendered piled masses of cloud
so pleasant in his eyes. The picture is thinly painted, and
seems little more than a sketch. It was done at Shobdon
Court whilst Gainsborough was on a visit to Lord Bateman.

We must mention yet one more view of an open glade
(Grosv. No. 193) in which sunset plays the principal part.
We look along a downhill road that winds westward to lower,
undulating country. Trees cast the foreground into a rich
brown shadow, contrasting finely with the golden light upon
the distant hills, and beaten back from the church-tower in
the hollow. All the living figures tell of the day's work
ended. A man bears his faggot homeward on his back,
whilst another rides his tired horses to their stable. All
these pictures express a somewhat plaintive, melancholic
attitude of mind, and are not what we should have looked

for from Gainsborough. The merry brook sparkling on its way, the grassy bank with its offering of spring flowers, the harvest-field and its golden treasure—these, and the like, are the subjects we should suppose would have attracted the laughter-loving heart of Gainsborough. But it was not so. Just as he became pathetic, and almost sad, in the presence of innocent childhood, so the pure face of nature likewise affected him. He was merry in the company of men—a rollicking boon companion—but alone he had serious moods. There was a depth of real solemnity in him. Had it not been so he would never have been the workman he was. The tenacity of purpose with which he adhered to his art and worked out its problems shows the stuff there was in him. In the last days of his life he confessed to Reynolds 'that his regret at losing life was principally the regret of leaving his art, and more especially as he now began to see what his deficiencies were, which he said he flattered himself, in his last works, were in some measure supplied.' He was one of a light and thoughtless society, and in its company he was as light and as thoughtless as any. But there were deep places in his heart, and a sight of nature availed to sound them.

IX.

Every now and again he painted in a gayer mood, as, for instance, in the 'Landscape, with figures at a pond' (Grosv. No. 136). The water is not really a pond, but a bay of a deep-

lying stream, shut in between high mud-banks and overlooked
by trees of different kinds. Their foliage is better distinguished
than usual, and it is possible to tell what kind of trees they
are. Broad daylight fills the air and crisps the bark of an old
pollard willow. A lad rides his pony to drink at the water
and talks the while with a maiden seated on the bank. Plants
in the foreground are painted with something of the early
minuteness, dock-leaves (Gainsborough's old favourites) being
particularly well drawn. Beyond the dark bank on the far
side is a view of a field, striped with sunlight and dotted with
sheep ; and there are scattered trees beyond, and a blue hill
above. The crisp touches of light which appear everywhere
give a character to the whole and are suggestive of the
handling of Constable.

Another picture of similar kind is the earliest edition
of the 'Cottage Door' (Grosv. No. 45). It is blotted
in in bright colours, with speedy skill. The chosen time
is the evening of an autumn day, and so the trees are
golden and flooded with golden light ; but the aspect of the
whole is gay as well as serene, and the cottage folk, dressed
in picturesquely patched garments, are happily chatting
together before their door. The elements of the scene are
few and simple. There is a gnarled, leafless trunk on the
right and a cottage behind it, overshadowed by and half buried
in foliage. A stream, crossed by a rustic bridge, flows
babbling round it, and a pollard willow leans over the waters
from the other bank. There is a tall tree on the left of
the foreground, leaning archwise towards the bare trunk on

the right; and there is a vista of sky and distant trees seen across the stream.   A very much earlier picture (Grosv. No. 208) contains some of these elements, a road and pond taking the place of the winding brook.   The idea, therefore, was one long resident in Gainsborough's mind.   In the last years of his life he returned to it again and again with increasing delight, and on a canvas, now the property of the Duke of Westminster (Grosv. No. 98), he painted the best realisation of it.   Here the elements are more closely fitted together, and the work is of a more decided and emphatic character.   The sun has gone further down and the evening is more advanced. A lingering brightness touches the horizon.   Higher up the clouds are dark and misty.   The only objects brightly illuminated in the foreground are the cottage-front and the group of cottagers, a mother and her six children receiving their evening meal.   The nodding masses of foliage are painted with a larger and heavier touch.   The water flows swifter and in greater volume, with less of rippling and more of racing.   The whole is painted with a greater fling, dashed into unity with a stronger hand.   The scheme of light and shade is almost Rembrandtesque.

In this picture, then, we may be said to possess the epitome of Gainsborough's landscape.   A glance at a collection of his drawings and etchings, such as that preserved in the Print Room of the British Museum, shows the compass of subjects that interested him.   Nine out of ten of his sketches are taken from little bits of rural scenery, in which foliation is the picturesque element ; cottages or churches buried amongst

GAINSBOROUGH.

The Watering Place.

trees, mounds or rough grass slopes surmounted by trees, banks overhung with trees. Almost always an old trunk lies or totters to its fall in the foreground. Whatever other objects are introduced are of a 'picturesque' character—old stone bridges, perhaps, or bony beasts, tattered gipsies, cracked cottages, or crazy walls. We scarcely ever find a view in which well-farmed country takes an important or even a minor part. Fertile meadows, too, are rare. Gainsborough preferred rough and broken country. He liked an open clearing in the midst of a wood, with a rough country road leading across it, and a pond lurking in the shadow at one side. He liked sandy commons and gravelly banks—anything, in fact, that was broken, uneven, or unkempt. He liked subjects the tone of which was in harmony with his own ragged technique. The 'Cottage Door' was exactly such a subject—the rough plank bridge, the well-worn cottage, the hurrying water, the broken ground in the wood behind, the old tree-trunk in front, the masses of foliage predominating over all, and the evening light infusing mellowness and mystery into everything ; all this suited Gainsborough to perfection, and enabled him to call into play the accumulated results of a lifetime of specialised study.

X.

GAINSBOROUGH's range of landscape did not embrace the sea, but an artist dwelling, as he did, by the banks of the Orwell, could not overlook the river and the estuary.

Walpole, speaking of the Academy Exhibition of 1781, says, 'Gainsborough has two pieces with land and sea, so free and natural that one steps back for fear of being splashed.' Perhaps the picture thus referred to is the Duke of Westminster's 'Coast Scene' (Grosv. No. 152). The foreground is a little cove beneath a cliff. On the windy beach two women are bargaining with a ragged fish-seller over the contents of his basket. The waves break crisply on the shore just behind them, and fishing-boats, leaning over to the wind, give to the distance the same aspect of life and movement with which the frolicsome foam and fluttering garments of the women animate the foreground. Round white clouds race across the blue sky, and a shepherd on the cliff-top shelters himself from the breeze. It is a sparkling picture, articulately suggestive of a single, delightful idea.* The general balance of light and mass in the composition of it was as much to Gainsborough's liking as that of the 'Cottage Door.' Probably it also was not arrived at without preliminary stages. The 'River Landscape' (Grosv. No. 137) shows the development of the idea in the artist's mind. It seems a little earlier than the 'Coast Scene,' and is therefore not quite so simple and direct. We have the same little bay in the foreground, with the same boat and its anchor lying stranded on the shore. In place of the cliff there is a castle rising out of trees upon a mound, whilst the fish-seller and his customers are supplanted by two men drawing in a net, to the intense delight of their excited dog. The water seems smooth in the distance, but it

* One of Morland's best landscapes is imitated from the 'Coast Scene.'

bears along a low, swelling ripple which crests itself and breaks into a merry foam about the legs of the wading fishermen.

Neither of the foregoing are pictures of sea-views. Water

SELLING FISH. BY G. MORLAND.

and shore in them alike tell of an estuary. The thundering storm-wave of the ocean no more belonged to Gainsborough than did the other grand and terrible sights of nature. There was little place for awe in his simple heart. Yet another landscape, different in composition but the same in spirit, remains to be mentioned. It is the 'Mouth of the Thames' (Grosv. No. 178). Once, again, we stand on a brown foreground, near some boats drawn up on the bank, and once again we have watermen and boys for our companions. The estuary opens before us and the farther low-lying bank recedes rapidly from view, humping itself into a gentle mound for distant emphasis. Fishing-boats are moving briskly about on the ruffled waters, some close at hand, others white on the horizon. A rounded mass of cumulus traverses the sky, parted per pale, sunlight and shade. These three pictures belong to the last years of Gainsborough's life, but in spirit they are one with the view of 'Landguard Fort,' which he painted for Thicknesse in his Ipswich days. The Fort stands on the end of a tongue of broken land with the reaches of the river all around it. Gainsborough himself is seated on an old tree-trunk in front, and there is a cart slowly descending along a rough road close at hand. In fact, the foreground is composed of the usual elements, and the river is, as usual, enlivened by a strong breeze which likewise hurries the clouds across the sky. Not that Gainsborough never painted calm water; he did so occasionally, as we shall immediately see; but in water, as in all other natural objects, he loved best the aspect of movement.

Perhaps he had just been attracted by a picture of Cuyp's when he sat down to paint the 'River Scene with Cattle' (Grosv. No. 180); at all events, the Cuyp influence is unmistakable. Again we are standing by the bank of a wide extending river. But it is evening; the breezes have gone to sleep, and the very clouds roll idly upon the dim horizon. The atmosphere is full of a mist so faint and tender that though it softens every object it is little less transparent than the clearest air. Some sailing boats lie near the shore with their sails flopping to and fro. Apparently the boatmen are taking market produce on board and two or three little row-boats are employed to help them. Inquisitive kine have collected about a jutting point of grass to survey the progress of affairs. They stand or lie picturesquely in front of the warm sunset. There is just enough of animation about the boatmen, just enough of movement about the row-boats, to give an undertone of liveliness to the scene. Everyone is quietly active, and the world's work is going forward even in this serene corner of land and water.

Much of the pleasant effect of the view arises from the picturesque manner in which the cattle are introduced. They are not there for their own sakes; they are elements of decoration, even as the plants by the hedgerow. Gainsborough often employed animals in that way. He sometimes painted dogs for their own sakes, and showed unusual skill in manifesting their individual characters, as, for instance, in a spirited little drawing of Tristram and Fox; but horses, cattle, sheep, goats, and donkeys, when they find their way into his pictures, do so in the character of picturesque elements. Even the fine chargers in the portraits of St. Leger and the Prince of Wales are little else than backgrounds to their owners; how much more then the bony Rosinantes of the highroad!

Animals frequently appear in Gainsborough's drawings, and the majority of his soft-line etchings of landscape scenes contain them in more or less prominent positions. One is devoted to a pathetically ragged group of donkeys, another shows a caravan of pack-horses going along a farm road. Cattle drinking at a pond, cattle crossing a bridge, these and the like subjects are common, but in none of them does the artist look at animals for their own sakes ; he does not concern himself with their habits, or make them his intimate friends. One of his best landscapes with cattle (Grosv. No. 77) may be taken as typical of the rest. It is a windy day, and so the beasts are lying on the ground grouped together under the lea of some low trees, prominent amongst which is the usual leafless trunk. The country is so nearly flat that the cattle hide all the distance from the beholder, and thus they become the subject of the picture. The painter's delight has been, not in the contemplation and rendering of the cow nature, but in the rich colouring of their expansive backs. He has brought them together, and made of them a fine surface decoration for the bleak field, their warm coats and comfortable forms contrasting pleasantly with the coldness of the surroundings.

All Gainsborough's animals (excepting once again the dog, for whom he had a natural fellow feeling) possess the quality of patience, which is indispensable to decorative objects. They have to be, and are, as patient as Caryatides. Horses plod along without so much as a rebellious whisk of their tails ; cows sit or lie like monuments ; donkeys have a look of even more than their proverbial endurance. Thus the artist shows his limitations. He selected from the visible world about him those objects and qualities which suited the requirements of his particular kind of art. He never went out of his way for anything new or startling. He was not, like Turner, on the watch for the manifestations of Nature's power. He did not look for storm and lightning, avalanche, fire, or flood. He did not ask for lofty mountains, and seldom even went so far as a waterfall. The scenes that he loved were the scenes of his own country-side, and he chose but a single group of them. In landscape, as in portraiture, he kept himself well in hand. He was not ambitious of wide power, and cared not that men should call him versatile. He wanted to get the best out of himself in the way that he felt he could work most naturally. Thus his style of expression and his mode of conception were always closely linked together. His hand gave the best form to the best thoughts of his heart. He was not an artist of great breadth and power, but within his own limits he was remarkably successful ; so that it may well be questioned whether any artist has ever come nearer than Gainsborough to the attainment of his own ideal.

LONDON :

Printed by STRANGEWAYS AND SONS, Tower Street, Upper St. Martin's Lane, W.C.

www.ingramcontent.com/pod-product-compliance
Lightning Source LLC
Chambersburg PA
CBHW032007010726
47493CB00007B/2306